TRAIN WRECK

THE HARRY STARKE NOVELS
BOOK 20

BLAIR HOWARD

COPYRIGHT

PROLOGUE

October 19th, 2018

Cooperman Industrial Park

North of Cleveland, Tennessee

The first few shots were wide, and the two young men ducked and weaved as they ran from the gunfire.

Dillon and his friend Brian, the one who'd started it all, the one who always had a million great ideas that couldn't be accomplished without him, hadn't expected to find anything in the old roundhouse other than a few rats and maybe a hobo or two. But even those were few and far between, at least in Cleveland, Tennessee.

More often than not, the empty buildings by the railyard were full of nothing but spiderwebs, trash, and dry rot. The real dangers were more of the falling-through-a-rotten-floorboard kind or stepping on a used needle.

But this... the guns, the chase, the mere presence of other people, was something neither of them had been prepared for, not even in the dark recesses of their minds where fight-or-flight reigned supreme.

Thankfully, those dark recesses didn't have the volume entirely turned down as Dillon pushed Brian ahead of him around a corner, somehow lost in a building that should have been as simple to exit as finding the nearest window. Not a pane of glass, not even a doorknob, as far as Dillon knew, still remained intact.

He stumbled over some scraps of wood. A busted-up chair, maybe, or firewood gathered on a cold winter night by one of the nomadic homeless passing through the outskirts of Cleveland. Dillon wanted to think that was what they'd stumbled across, but what he'd seen was the polar opposite of transience. What he'd seen was power.

Dillon couldn't help but wonder, as he ran for his life, how he and the klutz, the catalyst, the one who always fouled the mix, had been such good friends for so long. It was beyond him.

At times—most times, in fact—the guy was great, a willing participant, or at least the one most easily talked into things. Oh, Brian had ideas, all right. And they weren't bad ideas. Brian's ideas never were. But the execution... Somehow, it always left something to be desired.

He giggled a little, in spite of himself and the situation they were in. If they didn't find a way out of this rat hole, it wouldn't just be Brian's execution he needed to worry about; it would be his own, literally. Two heads would roll, of that he was certain. It would be a bad end to the adventure if he couldn't find a door, a way out, and quickly. And he was almost sure...

Yes. There. Up ahead, to the right. It was hard to make the distinction between the dark, midnight sky and the interior of the building, but he was almost positive those were stars he could see. Maybe a window, but really, it didn't matter. What mattered was getting outside. Getting away. What mattered was not being seen. Or at least not any more than they already had.

He lowered his shoulder and prepared, aimed himself at the wooden door and ran, hoping the latch had been busted off long ago.

The distance between them and the men with the pistols hadn't been much to begin with, and it certainly hadn't increased during the pursuit.

A bullet clipped the doorframe ahead of him, showering him with shards of wood.

He needed the door to give because if it didn't... Well, he didn't have another plan.

The side entry to the roundhouse burst open and the two young men stumbled out, barely keeping their balance as they skittered over the broken concrete sidewalk.

A toolshed, leaning in on itself since the last bad windstorm, had almost collapsed, the tired wood providing the only cover for some fifty yards in any direction. But still, the two made a beeline for it. Only seconds behind them, three men in dark suits, smoking pistols in hand, stepped into the open, spreading apart as they walked with a practiced, meticulous purpose. They moved forward cautiously but with a confidence and determination that implied it was not a matter of *if* they found their prey, but when.

Moving in an arrowhead formation, the three gunmen covered every degree of the yard and one another's back at the same time. Behind them, an older man, dressed in an impeccable suit, not only for these surroundings but for any surroundings, leaned in the doorframe, watching as his three associates moved purposefully across the yard, signaling to one another silently and spreading out as they closed in on the toolshed.

Two separated from the third, spacing themselves out to come at the building from both sides. The third, perhaps knowing his angle was the least likely, approached the rickety front door and put a hand on the knob.

It turned loosely in its casing, but before he could enter the outbuilding, a cry came up from behind the door, followed by the quick crack, crack, crack of three suppressed gunshots. He raced back around the corner of the building. At least this time they had a decent shot at the boys, whoever they were. Far from shooting fish in a barrel, tracking their targets inside the building had been more akin to firing at a black cat at the bottom of a well. Sure, they had an idea where they were, but it was mostly guesswork.

A yell... No. It was more of a screech... indicated that at least one of the bullets had found its target.

The gunman who'd been at the door to the toolshed turned and beckoned to the man leaning against the doorframe. He stepped forward and approached the shed. Whatever was taking place—whatever random, ill-conceived idea had interrupted his meeting—was about to become clear. Then it would be dealt with in whatever manner seemed most fitting. It seemed safe to say though, whatever manner that may be would almost assuredly include two bullets entering two skulls. His was not a party one should want to crash.

He sauntered toward the outbuilding, both irritated that an interruption had occurred at all, and pleased to have seen his men handle it so skillfully. One of them wasn't even his, but the three had worked in sync, almost as if they'd all attended the same hitman training school. He chuckled a little to himself at the thought: the United States military had served the purpose admirably.

Behind the shadow of the building, the moon shone down on the group of five men. One of them lay in a heap like a pile of discarded clothes. The growing pool of maroon around his head told that story well enough. Either one of the bullets had been lucky, or he'd simply been the easiest shot. But the impeccably dressed man only needed one of them alive, and that, for only a few more minutes.

The other young man was on his knees between the three gunmen, a deep gash running across the back of his forearm, another wound around his collarbone, and a third, from which he was ineffectually attempting to staunch the flow of blood, had struck him in his right side just below the ribcage. His breath was equal parts rasping and gurgling. Perhaps a punctured lung or blood in his stomach being retched up to his throat. But, as long as he could talk, it was of no concern.

The man approached the youth, squatting down in front of him so he could look him in the eye. The young man's eyes were wide, jittery, darting from man to man around the circle as if he were still expecting to find some means of escape. Fight or flight, to the bitter end.

"I think you'd better focus on me," the man said. "Clearly, you're in no shape to run, and even if you could, as your friend here has learned, you're not likely to be faster than a bullet."

The young man, perhaps in his mid-twenties, tried to focus on his captor.

"I must say," the man said, "when my men first informed me of your presence, I was expecting something a little more..." He searched for the proper word. "...experienced. But, unfortunately for you, though fortunately for me, it would appear we've both just had a case of bad luck. Then again, perhaps you've actually done me a favor." He glanced around at the three men, all standing with their weapons still in hand and pointed at the unlucky survivor of their ill-fated adventure. "I was curious to see how well, or not, these fellas would do in a time of crisis, and I must say, I'm quite impressed."

The young man wheezed, trying to form words, but bubbles of red spit were all he could form through his winces of pain.

The man held up a hand. "It's best you don't strain yourself too much. I just need a little information and then we'll be on our way." He held the young man's gaze for a moment, long enough to make sure the kid was focused, attentive. "What I need to know is fairly simple. First, what were you doing here?"

The young man struggled with his words, eventually bringing a thumb and forefinger to his mouth. "Smo... smoking."

The man raised an eyebrow. "Well, that's certainly not how it looked to me. Apparently, we weren't the only ones here on, shall we say, questionable business. Just smoking, is it?"

The kid mimed drinking from a bottle.

"Well, yes, I suppose the two do go hand-in-hand. At least you appear to be old enough for the latter." He looked up at the moon for a moment, laying out his thoughts in clear, concise lines. The two certainly didn't appear to be anything other than the ragtag youth he'd seen hanging out all over the city. Wasting time. Wasting opportunities. Contributing nothing outside of whatever menial job gave them enough money for a case of beer and a dime bag. It was unfortunate they'd chosen the roundhouse, of all places, to blow off some steam. But it also made things a little easier. And it wasn't as if they'd be missed, was it?

The man leaned a little closer to the injured captive. He waited until the boy's eyes focused and then asked him another question. "Do you know who I am?"

For a moment, the kid seemed unsure of how to answer, but finally, with a jerky nod, he indicated yes.

"I'm not surprised," the man said. "For what it's worth, either answer would've made no difference as to how this is going to go down. But I needed to know, just for... just for my own peace of mind, let's say."

The kid looked at him, clearly confused.

The man stood up and looked at one of his men. "Well, we certainly can't have this getting out."

He gave the man a curt nod, apparently a signal to carry on, then took a few steps back.

The gunman fired two shots, one into the youth's back, roughly where the heart would be. The other entered the back of his skull, just above the neck, ensuring there was no chance of survival. The body crumpled to the ground.

"Dig 'em in?" one of the men asked, holstering his weapon.

The man thought for a moment. "No. No sense in making it seem more mysterious than it needs to be. Missing persons get too much coverage these days. A couple of drunks on the tracks though..." He nodded toward the railroad embankment.

The gunman opened his mouth to say something when the low wail of a train engine cut through the night air.

"Drag them over to the tracks," the man said. "We've just enough time to let the train cover our tracks and then get back to business." He chuckled a little. "*Tracks!*"

The three gunmen exchanged a glance and then moved toward the bodies.

"Two of you should be sufficient," the man said. "Drape them over the tracks and hurry back. You..." He gestured to the third gunman. "You come with me. One can never be too careful."

Two of the gunmen grabbed the boys by the arms and, grunting, began to pull the bodies up the embankment toward the nearby railroad tracks. The man and his bodyguard turned and headed back to the building, already putting the incident out of their minds as if it had been of no more consequence than taking out the trash.

1

City Cafe Diner, Chattanooga, Tennessee

"It doesn't matter what you think," Kate said. "I had Samson trained to my needs within a week. Dogs are always going to be easier than kids."

I laughed. It was one of those things she'd been a firm believer in as long as I'd known her. Even when we'd been together—was that really eight years ago?— she'd sworn up and down she'd rather have a kennel full of dogs than try to raise a child. Especially if it was mine, she'd half-jokingly pointed out. And I had to give it to her; any kid that grew up with me as a dad wasn't likely to be the easiest one on the block. But at least now I had a counter-argument, Jade.

I slid my thumb across the face of my phone and pulled up some photos of my daughter and showed them to her.

"When Samson starts talking, you let me know."

"She's beautiful," Kate said, "but he communicates just fine and never screams, doesn't even bark, except when there are strangers at the door." She took a sip from her coffee.

I sighed. Why I continued to get into the same old debate was beyond me. Actually, come to think of it, I know exactly why. It gave me the perfect opportunity to be a doting father without coming off as overbearing or annoying. And, knowing Kate as I do, I'd almost bet this was exactly why she continued to bring it up. Neither of us was the touchy-feely type, but it wasn't like our hearts were made of concrete. We just needed to ease into... certain topics.

"Here you go," I said, tapping a short video clip. "Tell me Samson can do this."

I spun the phone around on the table so Kate could watch the thirty-second movie.

"Get SpaghettiOs in his hair? Oh, he does that all the time. He loves spaghetti any which way."

I laughed. "Fair enough. But look at that smile. Look at her eyes. Her little fists reaching out."

"Cats make muffins," she said. "Doesn't mean I want one."

"Fine," I said as I took the phone back, tucking it into my pants pocket. "We'll agree to disagree. I'll even do you one better. I don't ever expect to see Jade sniff out a kilo of cocaine in a toolshed."

Kate laughed. "Or a person."

I thought back to our last big case together. A kidnapping with all the trimmings: a missing person report, a canceled missing person report, a list of suspects as long as your arm and a possible serial killer father in the mix. It had been a fiasco, to say the least, and Samson had certainly played a key part in finding the girl once we got close. The dog even took a bullet for the girl in the final moments. Saved her life, judging from where I stood.

"He's back in tip-top shape, I take it?"

"You'd never know it happened," Kate said. "Slowed him down for a while, but if you want to talk about communicating, I swear that dog says more with his eyes than most people can with their mouths. The whole last week, it was like he was begging me to just get those bandages off and let him run."

"He's some kind of dog," I admitted. "You really lucked out with that one."

She laughed. "Be careful what you say here. Sounds like you're falling hard on the nature side versus the nurture side, and you've got, oh... another decade and a half of nurturing ahead of you."

I smiled, looking down at my coffee. "It's funny. Even that doesn't seem all that long."

"Don't get sappy on me now," she said. "You've got plenty of time for that when she gets her driver's license, or goes to prom, or..." She gave a false gasp. "...applies to an out-of-state college!"

"All right, all right." I held up my hands. "That's enough for now. I'm already trying to decide if those leashes they make for toddlers will fit a fifteen-year-old."

"Sounds like you're leaning toward team dog more than you realize," she teased.

"Oh, Amanda would never allow it. Says those leashes are inhumane. And I have to admit, I don't like the image of it much myself. But preschool isn't far off and I'm already dreading the idea of her being out there in the world."

"Spoken like a true cop," she said, then corrected herself. "I mean detective."

"Cop, ex-cop, whatever. I think it's just spoken like a father."

She nodded. "I'll give you that one. Although, considering the fathers you and I have come across, I think you might give yourself a little more credit."

It was as close as we usually came to complimenting one another, and a short, almost uncomfortable silence fell across our little table. I turned my mug on its saucer.

"So I haven't heard much out of you since the Hart thing," Kate said, referring back to the kidnapping case, the last time we'd really been in the trenches together. "You haven't needed me? Or there just hasn't been anything?"

Good old Kate. When things got too personal, there was always work. It was the perfect work-related friendship. But there were always the embers of our failed romance smoldering in the background. Oh, don't get me wrong. We were both well beyond it. Of what once had been, there was nothing left, other than the sometimes bitter memories.

Thankfully, my wife Amanda's work as a news anchor at Channel 7 TV provided her with just enough information to know what I had to deal with on a daily basis without getting her down in the gritty details. The work trained her in a way to expect information with a conclusion and no tiptoeing through the tulips on the way to it. She wanted an introduction and an ending so she could shelve her stories, not so she could lay awake all night wondering if she could've done more, if she had fouled everything up by being a moment too late.

Though being late wasn't always the worst thing in the world. I thought about my previous offices, demolished by a bomb that, had I been around for its detonation, would've been the end of Harry Starke, Private Investigator. It was almost the end of my career, regardless. Wives send their husbands out to work, no matter what the job, expecting there to be a certain amount of risk to it. Bank tellers get robbed. Firefighters turn toward the flames. Private investigators though, especially ones who take the cases like I do, tend to have a shadow of risk following them around no matter where they go.

But, with the new offices on Riverfront Parkway up and running, and the list of those actively seeking my demise shortening with every closed file, Amanda had somehow been able to reach down deep and put her faith in me, knowing that when I said I'd come home, I'd do everything in my power to keep that promise.

I looked back over at Kate, a strange mix of emotions in my gut. "I'm not leaving you out of anything. Just small-fry stuff lately. I figured you didn't want to be sitting outside some random hotel taking photos of a cheating spouse or trying to track down a deadbeat dad for child support."

"See?" she said. "You're not an adulterer or a deadbeat. You're nailing this father thing."

I smiled. "You know... It's funny. Before Jade, especially, and even before Amanda to a certain extent, a lull like this would've driven me crazy. Now I think, maybe these are the types of cases I should be taking. The boring ones. The low-key problems. You catch a guy with his pants around his ankles, and he's more likely to offer you hush money than he is to pull a gun on you."

"Depends on which guy," she replied, only half joking.

"Fair point," I said. "The point being, though, when we came up on that redneck reunion where they were holding Kelsey Hart, I thought maybe running toward the gunfire wasn't my best option."

"It's not always the case that it is," she said. "But that's the difference between you and the greenhorns I keep dealing with on the force. You know enough to see the difference between the smart move and the cowardly stupid one. Half the training I do is teaching these guys that nobody's gonna jump down their throats if they ask first and shoot second."

"The wisdom of age, is that it?" I laughed.

"Something along those lines."

I felt my phone buzz in my pocket and held up a finger while I pulled out the device and checked the screen.

"Text message," I said, apparently with more of a sigh than I realized.

"Wisdom isn't the only thing that comes with age," Kate said. "Curmudgeonly old man resistance to change is in there too."

"Hey," I said indignantly. "I'm not old. I'm still in my forties."

She looked hard at me.

"I know, I know," I said as I flipped open the message. "It's from Jacque. 'What time can you be in the office?' She couldn't just call and ask? Now I've got to write her back. We're already wasting time."

"Maybe she thought you were busy."

I laughed. "Jacque knows where I'm going even before I know myself, most times. Ten bucks says she could've driven over early and been waiting at the table for us."

I found the phone icon and texted her back. Punching the little letters—and then inevitably changing things when the phone thought it knew what I wanted to spell. It seemed about as tedious as finding hay in a needlestack, so I called her instead.

"Hey," Jacque said, answering on the first ring. "I don't know why I texted. Didn't want to interrupt a friendly chat, I guess."

I smiled and put the phone on speaker. "What do you think I'm doing?"

Jacque sighed, and I could perfectly picture her looking up at the ceiling, running through potential options. "If I had to guess," she said, "considering it's a Monday morning and you're not here, but you didn't say you'd be at home, and given that we haven't had a whole lot to do since the Kelsey Hart Hillbilly Hoedown, I'd guess you met up with Kate for breakfast somewhere to see if there's anything more juicy than a philandering husband happening in this town."

I gestured toward the phone.

"Hi, Jacque," Kate said, leaning in. "You just cost me ten bucks."

Jacque laughed. "Buy his coffee and call it even. We need him back here."

"What's the news?" I asked.

"Kind of a tricky one," she said. "I've got two guys in here wanting to talk to you, but only you. Apparently, my charm has no effect on them."

"Did they say what they need?"

"Outside of needing you in the flesh, no. I know they drove in from Cleveland this morning, and they don't look like they're moving from their chairs until you get here."

"What is that?" Kate said. "Half an hour? Forty-five minutes?"

"Depending on the traffic and time of day, yes, something like that," Jacque replied. "We didn't really have much get-to-know-you banter. Said they wanted Harry Starke and settled in."

Kate looked at me, her eyebrows raised.

"All right," I said. "Tell them I'll be there shortly. See if you can find out what they want. Let them know you'll likely be working with me."

"Oh, I tried that one already, Harry. I told them I was your partner, but I think they have to hear it from the horse's mouth."

I scoffed. Jacque was one of the best I'd ever worked with, which was saying a lot, considering I only hired the best to begin with. And she is my partner. She owns twenty-five percent of the business. "Tell them I'll be there in fifteen minutes then."

"Take your time." She laughed. "Call it a rudeness tax."

"I'll see you shortly," I said and ended the call.

"Mysterious beginnings," Kate said, unhooking her bag from the back of the chair. "Sounds like you may be pining for a hotel stakeout sooner than you expected."

"You may be right," I said, standing up and tossing a few bills on the table. "Cleveland isn't exactly lacking in law enforcement."

She looked at the table. "I thought I was paying for your coffee?"

"You can get it next time," I said.

"All right, Harry," she said as we walked to the door. "But keep me posted on this one. My curiosity is piqued."

"You just want to know why they came to me and not you." I laughed, holding the door open.

"Cleveland's outside my jurisdiction, and Whitey's," she responded. "But you're right. What kind of case needs the famous Harry Starke and no one else?"

Whitey, as she called him, is the sheriff of Hamilton County. Cleveland is just to the north in Bradley County.

"I guess I'm about to find out," I said.

I waited until she'd gotten in her unmarked cruiser and pulled out of the lot, then headed in the opposite direction, my mind already running through options of what exactly could be awaiting me at the end of the short drive to the office.

2

Monday, 9:45am

As usual, what was waiting for me, as soon as I stepped through the door, was Heather, my head of investigations, with a smile on her face and a mischievous look in her eyes that said she already had some news and wanted to bring me up to speed on a case she was working.

"You were right," she said, stepping away from the coffee station in the large foyer.

"That's always a great way to start a conversation," I said. "What am I right about this time?"

"Well, I suppose technically Sandra Matters was right, if you're going to be cocky about it."

"But I agreed with Mrs. Matters."

She rolled her eyes. "Okay, you were both right, then. The husband and the secretary. But I mean, as cliche as that is, we may as well say 'the butler did it.'"

"Which is why I read your resume before I hired you," I said. "The last thing I need is someone thinking I hire my team based on anything besides credentials."

Heather is the picture of health and good looks. Even after seeing her in action and reading about her time with the Georgia Bureau of Investigation, I'd been hesitant. Because she was right. The boss and the secretary, the boss and the intern, the boss and whoever. It opened up the possibility for problems that, in a job like ours especially, could not be tolerated. But I knew when hiring Heather—because she'd told me, not through any guessing on my part—that she prefers women.

"Well, anyone looking into it that closely would've been well aware that you aren't exactly *my* type, sir." she said, grinning at her own joke.

"And a good thing." I laughed. "We'd fall apart without you."

"Aw shucks." She smiled, though her false modesty was only partial. Heather knew as well as anyone else that our team worked because we were fine-tuned. We knew how to rely on one another, we knew that we had to, and it was a delicate balance that no one wanted to shake.

"What's the story on our mystery men?" she said, changing the subject.

"I don't have the slightest idea," I said. "You pick up anything?"

"Nope." She stirred her coffee a little. "Jacque was the first one they saw when they came through the door and the rest of us didn't even get a wave."

I nodded. "All right. Well, stick close. Something tells me this isn't going to be as simple as the Matters thing."

"I could use a change of pace."

"Be careful what you wish for. Come on."

I walked into my office to find Jacque in the chair behind my desk, the two men sitting across from her in a pair of cushioned wooden seats. I tried to get a feel for the room as I entered. The two men—both looked to be around thirty and working class—weren't a pair I would've looked at twice if I'd passed them on the street. One had a beard, the other didn't have as much as a shadow, and other than the fact that they both seemed exceedingly nervous, they could've been two pals from Cleveland on a day trip to Costco's, assuming they'd gotten time off at the factory, or wherever they used their hands. The jeans and workshirts were enough for anyone to see they didn't spend their days behind a computer, in spite of the fact that the clean-shaven man had a rolled manila file folder in his hand, which he kept tapping on his knee.

"Gentlemen," I said, taking off my jacket and hanging it on a peg on the wall. "I apologize for the wait. For future reference, Miss Hale here is as much a part of this team as anyone else, so you don't need to mince words around her." I gestured for her to stay put and sat myself on the corner of the desk. "In fact, she'll be here for the remainder of this meeting, as will my chief investigator Heather Stillwell." I nodded to Heather, who went and sat down at the back of the room.

"We didn't mean no disrespect," the man with the folder said. "But yours is the name we knowed."

I nodded. Mine was the name on the business, after all. Still, I wanted them to see Jacque behind the desk to drive home the point. This was going to be a team deal or no deal at all.

"Speaking of names," I said. "You know mine. Care to introduce yourselves?"

"I'm Jacob Harper," the man with the file said. Then, gesturing with said file to his friend, "This here's Blake McDaniel. We come on accounta we weren't getting nowhere with nothing there in Cleveland."

I raised an eyebrow. "Cleveland's got a top-notch police force. Chief Snow's a friend of mine," I said. "I'm not sure what you think I'll be able to find or tell you that they haven't already."

"Well, the finding's a part of it," the bearded one, Blake, said.

I glanced to Jacque; she already had a legal pad and pen ready.

"All right," I said. "Tell me a little about what we're looking for, and we'll see what we can do."

The two men exchanged a glance and Jacob ceased tapping the file on his knee, choosing instead to wring it between his hands.

"Well, it's like this," Jacob said, apparently the spokesperson for the two. "Blake and me, we been pallin' around for a good long while. Growed up next to one another. Went to school together. Work together an' all that. But we each of us got little brothers—well, not so little, really—who done just about the same."

"Maybe not workin' so much," Blake interjected.

"Right. Yeah. Well, they, uh..." Jacob shook his head, clearing his thoughts. "That ain't really the point. My brother, Dillon, and his brother, Brian, are thick as thieves. Never see one without the other most days. And three-and-a-half years ago, come Friday, they both go missing. They go out for a beer and they don't come home, which ain't entirely out of the ordinary when they get on a tear, but they didn't show up none the next morning neither."

"I'm assuming you filed missing persons reports," I said.

"Didn't need to," Jacob said. His voice cracked slightly. "They *was* found." Without even looking at Jacque, I knew she was thinking the same thing I was. It was almost verbatim what had happened with the Hart girl. She was missing, then supposedly found, then missing again.

"And where are they now?"

"Graveyard," Blake said, his tone curt, his emotions clamped down.

"I see," I said. "Where exactly were your brothers found?"

"Tracks," Blake spoke again, as if there were only one possible set of tracks I could think of.

"The rail line that runs through town," Jacob clarified. Almost as if he'd just realized he'd been holding it, he held the file folder out to me. "They was both found aside the tracks, what was left of 'em. Folks say they just went on a bender, got their selves in it a little too deep. Passed out on the tracks and then the train, well..." He looked out the window as if trying to hide the moisture in his eyes.

"All right," I said, opening the file, hoping to get on more stable, less emotional ground. "Let's see what you've got in here."

What he had was disappointing at best. There was a news article torn, not clipped, from the Cleveland Daily Banner, the least appealing aspect of it being the date at the top. It was from almost four years ago. The only other sheet inside was a hand-written list of names that, at the moment, meant nothing to me. I scanned the article, though it said very little Jacob hadn't just explained. The boys were found on the tracks; the tox report came back with high levels of alcohol and marijuana. It seemed pretty cut and dried, and I told them so.

"This feels pretty straightforward, fellas," I said. "What is it that brings you to me now?"

"Look." Blake leaned forward, subconsciously stroking at his beard. "This is between me and y'all, all right?" He waited for me to nod, then looked at Jacque, who also nodded, and then continued. "I ain't saying I never rolled up a joint in my life, and Lord knows I've seen every bit as many empty bottles as full ones, but in all my days, I ain't never been so snockered I'd plumb pass out on a set of rails. Now you're gonna tell me *both* them boys did? I don't think so!"

I glanced back down at the files. "The report seems to indicate that," I said. "Granted, I agree it seems a little odd both your brothers would've done so, but, well, as you said, folks get snockered. They black out. I don't know what your brothers were into or how much they were used to. Maybe they just had an off night. Maybe they had every intention of moving on."

Blake looked at me. His eyes were not the cold, angry points I expected, but almost hurt.

"Maybe they did," he said, "but for the sake of our fathers, would you at least look into it? Don't no man deserve to find out he lost his boy on accounta he didn't have the tol'rance he thought he did, or the good sense to not sleep on the railroad tracks."

For the first time, Jacque spoke up. "We'll look into it," she said. "In fact, given the little amount of information you've been able to gather, there may still be plenty more out there waiting for us." She looked at me. "Is there a tox screen in there?"

I held up the file for her to see. "Just a clipping and these names."

"Folks you might wanna talk to," Jacob said.

I nodded. "The medical examiner would be one I'd be interested in."

"She's on there," Jacob said. "But don't expect much outta her."

"That's why we come to you," Blake said. "Folks don't have much trouble blowing off a couple wrench-turners, but we was hoping you might have some better luck."

"We'll do the best we can," Jacque said, standing up. "And we'll be in touch. If you come with me, Heather will get your information..."

The door closed behind them and I reclaimed my seat behind the desk. All the mystery that had surrounded these two men seemed to vanish in a puff of air. Of course they want closure on the death of their brothers. Of course your mind wants to find options that are more palatable than the reasons given. But aside from how they were planning to scrape together the money for this investigation, I couldn't see much in the file—what little there was of it—worth pursuing.

A moment later, Jacque stepped back into the room. "I know what you're going to say," she said, speaking quickly before I had a chance. "And I'm not saying you're wrong."

"All right," I said. "I'm listening."

"There was a case a few years ago," she said, taking one of the chairs across from me but only sitting on the edge. "Female, about twenty, found dead on the railroad tracks. Tox came back with an almost ludicrously high blood alcohol level. Turns out she'd been at some kind of party, maybe a hazing, though nobody ever came forward about that particular aspect. The point is, getting so drunk you pass out on the tracks isn't impossible. Uncommon, unfortunate, sure. But it's not like you can pick where you pass out any more than people pick where they have seizures or strokes."

"Okay," I said. "But you're making my point."

"I am," she said. "I think it is entirely feasible that a young man could drink too much, especially mixed with marijuana or other substances, and pass out on the tracks. For all we know, he tripped on one rail, hit his head on the other, and knocked himself unconscious. With nobody there to help him up, the train comes, and that's all she wrote."

"If there's nobody there to help him up," I said, seeing her point.

"Exactly."

I sighed. "All right. They're right: two of them ending up on the tracks? It stretches the bounds of probability more than a little, don't you think? No matter. Don't answer that. Rally the team in the conference room. We'll look into it. But make sure you get the retainer up front. I'm still not convinced."

She grinned at me. "I got it before they left."

The team was seated in their usual places around the large table in the conference room. It wasn't as if we had assigned seating, just the tendency of people to fall into familiar habits and stick to them. This type of predictability was something I depended on in this type of business. Patterns, even the breaking of patterns, stand out. Before the full team had even arrived, empty spots awaited the particular person who, for whatever reason, had laid claim to it.

Once they were settled, Jacque ran them through the general overview of the case, fielding the standard questions we'd all grown accustomed to asking at the beginning of any investigation. The old who, what, when, where, why and how. Why was usually the trickiest, though the other five had all been known to throw some curveballs in the past as well.

"I mean, that can't be all of it," Tim, our resident computer genius, was saying. "Sure, maybe these two guys didn't have the tox screen with them, but it's not like there just isn't one. And if there was some kind of snafu that left it unfiled..." He whistled. "Everybody makes mistakes, but a time gap like this is going to come back to haunt somebody."

"Right," Jacque said. "The guys don't say there wasn't a file, but they do claim they weren't given it by the ME, though they didn't go into details either. Maybe it was just a case of ruffled feathers, but if we're going to look into this, we need everything we can get."

"Meaning?" Tim almost looked hopeful. Behind his almost squirrelly appearance was a brilliant and dedicated mind. More often than not, when I saw this gleam in his eyes, I knew I'd find him at his desk when I returned in the morning, having either taken nothing more than catnaps or, more likely, not slept at all in front of the keyboard.

"Meaning," Jacque said. "I want anything you can find about this case, other than this." She held up the newspaper article. "But if you're feeling froggy, print off the full day's edition as well. May not hurt to see what else was happening in Cleveland around this time. My history is decent, but not for small towns three years ago."

"But what if it comes back like they said?" Heather asked. "I mean, at this point, yes, it's unfortunate, but to be frank, people do stupid things. Drunk people do even stupider ones."

Across from her, TJ leaned in. He was by far the oldest person on our team and had, without a doubt, lived the hardest years. His military background, his time living the homeless life, if I should've turned to anyone right away, it should've been TJ.

"I'm not gonna disagree with you there," he said. "Drunk folks are worse than drug addicts a lotta the time. But in all my days on the street, I've never seen two fellas pass out at the same time in the same place. Especially in a place like that."

"Maybe it was a game," Tim said, getting all eyes on him again. "I mean, I'm not saying it's a good game, but you know how videos work. One person posts something stupid, then someone else has to out-do it. Suddenly you've got a viral disaster on your hands. Train jumping is hardly a new idea."

"You think they just tried to beat it?" I asked.

He shrugged. "I don't know what they were thinking. But it makes more sense to me than two guys making a suicide-by-train pact."

Jacque held up a hand. "Look, right now, we can pretty well consider anything a possibility. I just want everyone in the loop as we move forward. Tim, anything you find, you do the same. I know this isn't a world-shaking case, but those two men we saw earlier lost their brothers, and we at least owe it to them to give it our best effort."

"On it," Tim said.

"Before we get carried away," Heather said, "TJ and I have some loose ends to tie up. Keep us posted, but I'd say we're sidelined until the day after tomorrow, most likely."

I nodded. "That's fine. Jacque, you and I can run point on this for a day or two, surely. The rest of you get after what needs doing." As the team dispersed, I thought for a moment and then looked over at Jacque. "Who else do we know at the Cleveland PD besides Chief Snow?"

She was already scrolling through her phone, her list of contacts probably nearing the length of the old-fashioned paper phone books by this point. "That's what I was trying to see..." Her finger flicked the screen. "I feel like there should be someone, but there aren't any names springing to mind."

I leaned forward in my chair. "I was just thinking the same thing."

"You want me to call them?"

"Actually," I said, remembering why I left the Chattanooga force. "Let's do things a little differently. Part of the fun of being a PI is that we don't have to jump through the hoops anymore."

"Surprise visit?"

"It's only forty-five minutes," I said. "And I know your schedule is open."

She laughed. "Give me five minutes and I'll meet you at the car."

"Done."

3

***

Monday, 12:05pm

IT WAS JUST AFTER NOON WHEN WE ARRIVED IN Cleveland and, as we didn't have any appointments, Jacque and I made a pit stop at the Little Old Fort to grab a bite to eat and run over our game plan.

"Busy," she said, looking out the large glass windows onto 25th Street.

"Yes," I said as we watched the traffic. "It's growing fast. I remember the days when—"

"I'm sure you do," she replied with a cheeky grin.

Just then the waiter came over to take our order. Jacque ordered a hamburger steak, mashed potatoes, green beans and carrots with banana pudding to follow. I swear she eats like a lumberjack and still always looks like she could use a few extra pounds. Oh, don't get the wrong idea. She's slim, trim and fit. It's just that... Oh, never mind. Me? I ordered a burger, no fries. I don't need the extra pounds.

"Small-town folks can be talkative," I said before taking a bite. I swallowed, took a sip of my iced tea, then said, "Ready to share the latest gossip. You've seen it, right?"

She laughed. "Oh, I've seen things, Harry. And what I'm seeing right now is a white man forgetting we aren't in the big city. I don't know Cleveland from a bump on a log, but I know you and me sitting together in a small town like this is probably already making the rounds." She leaned in conspiratorially. "You think it'll make it better or worse if they find out the brown girl is a lesbian?"

I shook my head, grinning. It was impossible to not laugh when Jacque set her mind to making you do so. "I think you should consider taking one note from small-town life then: some things are best kept to yourself. But if you're so sure everyone is already gossiping, why not add some fuel to the fire?"

She looked at me, an eyebrow raised, and I laughed again. "Not like that. I mean, we're here for information, so let's get started. We've got one current resident heading back to our table in a few minutes. Let's see what she knows."

"Catherine?" she asked.

I gave her a puzzled expression.

"It's on her nametag, Harry." She shook her head. "And you call yourself a private investigator."

I rolled my eyes. "I can't be on top of it all the time. That's why I have you guys."

"Mm-hm."

Nevertheless, when our waitress returned, Jacque was more than up to the task.

"Catherine," she said, looking up at her. "We have a question for you if you have a moment."

Catherine looked to be around sixty. She frowned, then smiled and said, "What's on your minds?"

"A few years back," Jacque continued, "two young men were found on the railroad tracks outside of town. We were wondering if you'd heard anything about that?"

"Like, they were dead?" she asked. "Kinda gruesome for meal-time talk, ain't it?"

Jacque looked down, almost sheepish. "I suppose you're right, but we're in a bit of a rush."

"I thought so," she said, smiling down at us. "City folk, aren't you? Always in a rush. You're talking about those two who got hit by a train at the old Cooperman Industrial Park. Yeah, I heard about it. We all did, but all I know is they was drunk, and I'll tell ya, boys around here are always findin' new ways to get up to trouble every time you turn around. Cooperman used to be where they went to work. Now it's where they go to do Lord knows what all with Lord knows who. You couldn't get me out there if you paid me."

"Is it dangerous?" Jacque asked, and I knew what she was thinking. If the place already had a reputation, we might have a few strings to pull.

"Well, yeah," the woman said. "It's in a rare state now. Buildings falling down, rusty nails, rats, hoboes, nasty. You try and walk through there to get home without a weapon and you're liable to catch something that'll turn you inside out. Safer walking the rails than that place." She paused for a moment, seeming to realize what she said. "Or at least, most times, I reckon. I'm surprised they haven't pulled it all down."

"So, what you're saying is, it's not safe to even walk through the industrial park?" Jacque asked.

"More like I got better things to do than wander around abandoned buildings," Catherine said. "I don't mean no disrespect to the dead, but folks don't go headin' out that way for their Bible studies, if you understand me. Them boys got hit by a train. My best guess is they was so blind drunk they couldn't see straight enough to pick out which train they needed to dodge." She looked back and forth between us. "Food all right?"

I nodded and Jacque thanked the woman, who promptly disappeared somewhere into the kitchen.

"So what do you make of that, super sleuth?" Jacque said, spearing a chunk of hamburger steak with her fork.

"Other than the fact that she'd be one hard-hearted grandmother, not much," I said. "But what I did see was what was missing."

Jacque glanced at me briefly, reaching for the hot sauce in the condiment rack.

"Surprise," I said. "She didn't act surprised. And she didn't act as if the idea of the two kids dying like that was something she couldn't believe."

"So you're back to saying it was an accident?" she said.

"I've been saying it was an accident all along," I replied. "But I'm committed enough to see it through, at least for now."

I shook my head and sighed. "The police department is just a few minutes away on Church Street. Hopefully, we'll find something with a little more meat on it there."

"City folks," Jacque mocked the woman's accent perfectly. "Always in a hurry. Let a gal enjoy her food."

We parked across the street and walked in through the glass doors. The receptionist looked up from her computer monitor and said, "Hep you?"

Unfortunately, as I tried to explain why we were there, the woman became less interested in talking with us. And once she realized we weren't there to report a crime or a missing person, she fell into what was obviously a well-rehearsed and all-too-familiar refrain.

"I'm sorry, but you'll need to make an appointment..." yadda, yadda, yadda.

"I completely understand," I said, switching on my best smile at her. "I run a business myself, so I can appreciate the need for uniformity and scheduling. We were just hoping that, since we'd driven up here, you might be able to persuade the chief to give us a few minutes. It doesn't have to be right this moment, just maybe in the next few hours."

"I'm sorry, but unless you're a police officer..."

"I'm ex-Chattanooga PD, homicide," I replied. "I'm Harry Starke, a licensed private investigator."

The woman's eyebrows went up. "Harry Starke? I... I... Let me see what I can do."

I turned and grinned at Jacque. She rolled her eyes.

After a quick phone call, the door behind the receptionist opened and a female sergeant stepped out and said, "If you'll follow me, Mr. Starke."

Chief Charlie Snow was seated behind his desk, but he stood and walked around it, his hand out and said, "Harry. It's been a while. What brings you to Cleveland? Nothing good, I'm sure."

"Charlie," I said, taking his hand. "It's good to see you. You're looking good."

He pulled a face and said, "Holding my own, I guess. But look at you... But who's this?"

"My business partner," I replied. "Charlie Snow, Jacque Hale."

They shook hands, Snow grinning. He looked at her, then at me, then at her again and said, "I'm in the wrong business."

He let go of her hand and said, "So, sit down. What can I do for you? Which case is it this time?"

"That's a strange question, Charlie," I said. "What d'you mean?"

"Well, as you know, I was appointed chief less than three years ago..." he began thoughtfully, then sighed. "It's part of the transition, I suppose. Cold cases, loose ends left untied, that sort of thing."

"I see," Jacque said.

"Within your window, then, I take it?" Snow asked.

"Not quite, but you know what they say." She grinned. "Close enough for government work."

Snow laughed. "So tell me; what brings you here then?"

I began to explain, but before I got far, he held up a finger, stood up and went to one of two large file cabinets to the left of the office door.

"I was assistant chief then..." He hesitated, looked at Jacque and said, "I don't want you to think I'm being rude, but I inherited these two cabinets full of cases that are either incomplete, open, or simply haven't been filed away properly in the closed case section. And, if I'm being brutally honest, I've not given them the kind of attention I probably should have. But," he said and sighed, "there are only so many hours in a day."

He flicked through the files before pulling one. Then he returned to his seat behind his desk, glanced inside it briefly, closed it, then leaned forward and handed it to me.

"That's what we've got," he said, leaning back in his chair, elbows on the arms, fingers steepled together in front of him.

"Pretty slim," he said. "If you were hoping for a plethora of information, I'm afraid you're going to be disappointed."

I opened the file and, just as he'd said, I was more than a little deflated when I saw how sparse the paperwork was.

The chief's phone buzzed and he had a short chat. The man was nothing if not transparent, taking calls in front of us and freely handing files over.

"I'm afraid I'll have to cut our meeting short," he said after ending his call and standing up.

I moved to do the same when he gestured for me to remain seated.

"No, no," he said. "Stay as long as you need to, Harry. You're doing me a favor looking into this. In fact..." He reached down to a small stand on his desk. "Here, take my card. If you need anything, have any questions, whatever it may be, that's my cell number there. I'll be happy to steer you in the right direction or tell you if I'm stumped myself." He laughed. "I'll send Sergeant Williams in to keep you company. You can leave the file with her... Gotta go."

"We appreciate it, Charlie," I said.

"And I appreciate the help," he said. "Best of luck. Call me."

He pulled the door closed, and Jacque and I exchanged a glance.

"Better take advantage of it while we can," she said.

I stood up so we could spread the papers out on the desk so Jacque could snap photos of them with her phone.

While a lot of it was standard, boilerplate forms, filled out and stamped in all the right places, I was pleased to see the reports from the medical examiner. Or at least what should have been reports.

"And I thought I had bad handwriting," Jacque said, holding the paper closer to her eyes, then farther away. "I know there's that stereotype about doctors, but wow. This is almost illegible."

"Can you make anything out?" I said as I flicked through the logsheets and officer reports.

"Brenda something or other... Po...Polaski? That a name?"

I laughed a little. "Probably close enough. How many MEs do you think are in this town? We only have one in Chattanooga."

"Well, more than one, I think," she replied. "This one's a private contractor. Unusual, don't you think?"

"Really?" I glanced over at the paperwork, though, as Jacque had pointed out, it was almost impossible to read anything.

"A private ME without much to say," Jacque said as she flipped the page over and back. "These aren't even full reports. Just basically notes saying she did it. At least from what I can decipher."

"What's the tox report say?" I asked.

"'Completed.' That's what it says."

"That's it? Nothing else?"

"Nope." Jacque shook her head and looked me in the eye. "That's all she had to say about it."

I looked out the window at the buildings across the street, not really seeing them. Sloppy handwriting by a doctor is the norm. But a private ME, well, it wasn't normal, but it wasn't unheard of either. An incomplete tox file when the cause of death was solely based on the tox screen... now that was a problem.

"Looks like we need to make an appointment with Dr. Polanski," I said.

"Polaski," Jacque corrected me, jotting the name down in her pocket notebook. "Polanski was the movie guy. Sharon Tate? Remember?"

I nodded. "Noted. Add these names to your list while you're at it. Sergeant Louise Baker, lead detective. And..." I ran my finger down the page. "Mark Johnson, engineer. Bobby Wallace, conductor."

Jacque wrote, then waited, pen poised over the paper. "That's it?"

"That's it," I said, gathering up the papers and putting the file in the middle of the chief's desk. "One detective, two witnesses. I guess, considering it was the middle of the night in the middle of nowhere, these three and your ME aren't a bad start."

"So who's first?"

"Nobody," I said, opening the map app on my phone. "First, we're going to the tracks. I hope you've had your tetanus booster."

4

Monday, 2:15pm

WE DROVE SLOWLY OUT TO THE NORTH END OF TOWN AND then made a right into what I assumed was an industrial park. The signs, if there ever had been any, were long gone, as were most of the buildings. Only the shells of brick-built buildings remained.

I parked in what once had been a large parking lot, now an overgrown, broken asphalt lot, weeds growing up through the cracks and all but obscuring where the faded yellow lines used to be. Off to our left were a few single-story outbuildings, a large roundhouse, a water tower from the earliest of the early days, and a two-story warehouse; at least, I thought it was a warehouse, but who knew.

I climbed out of the car and started toward the tracks, Jacque keeping pace beside me while stumbling over chunks of dirt in her heels and moving her phone around as she walked.

"Maybe one thing at a time," I said. "I don't need you cracking your head open."

"Then hold up a minute, damn it." She zoomed in on the picture on her phone, then out again, looking at our surroundings. "All right," she said and pointed, "this way."

"How about this way first?" I said.

I led us up to the rails, which even with their narrowly spaced ties, provided at least a somewhat more stable walking surface.

"This isn't going to be precise," she said. "The crime scene photographer wasn't standing on the tracks. Probably because he had clear evidence of why it wasn't too smart to hang out on them. But," she said as she flicked back and forth between several photos, "we should be close." She stepped out from between the rails and walked back a few paces, eyeing the sparse landmarks around us.

"Okay," she said. "Go on about ten feet that way, and best as I can tell, you oughtta be right on the spot where the bodies were found. Darn close anyway."

I looked down at where I stood. I'd known better than to expect any evidence. After this long out in the weather and with continuous traffic over the last four years or so, anything that might have been useful would have long since been destroyed, buried, or blown away. But getting a feel for the place, seeing how things lined up, well, that's something I always do, and it's usually worth it.

I looked around. There was a small, dilapidated toolshed to my left, Jacque's right. From the look of things, a strong breeze would send it toppling, and I hoped we wouldn't have to go inside. If anywhere would have the rusty nails Catherine feared so much, the shed would be it.

Behind Jacque was the roundhouse, still surprisingly sturdy looking. The windows had been busted out. More than one delinquent with a spray can had left his mark, but the structure itself appeared indifferent to the abuse.

A warm breeze blew across the park. If we'd been out west, I would've expected to see a tumbleweed rolling across the broken asphalt.

"All right," I said. "Come over here. Let's take a look at those photos."

Jacque came over and held the phone out, one hand shielding the screen from the sun. She flicked back and forth between the relevant shots, double-checking our position and looking down at the rails and ties at our feet. "I feel like we're several years too late," she said.

"Maybe," I said. "Hold on. Go back to the last shot."

She flicked across the screen and held the phone over to me. I used my fingers to zoom in and then look around at the details of the photo.

"I think..." I began, zooming back out. "Maybe what we need to see isn't here at all. And probably wouldn't have been once the scene was cleaned up."

"What do you mean?" She had her feet apart, hands on her hips, her head cocked to one side.

"Look at these bodies," I said, turning the phone so she could see more clearly. "What stands out to you?"

The photos were pretty damn gruesome. Heads, arms and feet had been severed, bodies crushed. "Well, the placement, for one thing," she said. "It looks like they were on their backs, necks on that rail, feet... stretched out, like... Harry, this wasn't an accident. They either committed suicide or they were already dead when the train hit them."

I grimaced. What she was saying made sense. "Yup. If they'd been dragged across the tracks..."

"Yeah. Like this," she said as she held her hands up over her head. "Legs on one side, arms up over the other. Torso and thighs between the rails. What's the width of the rails? Any idea?"

"Yep, I know that one. Standard gauge is four-feet-eight-and-a-half inches. If the kids were anything like their brothers, they'd have been more than tall enough. Okay, this is good," I continued. "But what else do you see? Think about where we are."

She was close behind me, staring down at the photo. It took her a minute before she said, "I don't know, Harry. What's left of the arms and legs just show where the train severed them from the body, and the bodies look... awful... wait." She took the phone out of my hand, zooming in and out as I had done just a few moments before. "Oh," she said. "Oh that's straight grisly."

"It doesn't make sense, though, does it?" I asked. "And yes, grisly, to say the least. But as far as being killed by a train, not as grisly as maybe it should be. The majority of the blood is *between* the rails. And if you look..." I zoomed in again, moving the focus of the photo to the rails. "Even where the limbs were severed, there was very little blood on the line, or on either side of the line; significantly less than you'd expect, wouldn't you say?"

"Well, to be fair, we didn't cover a lot of death-by-train cases in my criminology courses, but logic seems to be on your side."

"Exactly," I said, kneeling down in the gravel on the ties. "If these two guys were alive, or even, shall we say, intact, when the train came, there would've been significant spray. There should be blood all over the place. But there's not. The vast majority of it is in the one spot you'd least expect... reasonably least expect. It's all between the rails, right about here." I pointed to a spot on one of the ties about a foot from the rail on the eastern side of the tracks. "The rails should've taken the majority of the blood, which would've then run down this way." I ran my thumb along the iron line. "Into the gravel, on the ties, and..." I pointed off to both sides. "There, there, there, and there, and maybe even there. For it to pool here..." I looked at her expectantly.

You have to understand that Jacque, though she's not a trained investigator, is smart as a whip. She's Jamaican by birth, thirty-three years old, but looks nineteen. She's tall—five nine—has skin the color of coffee and cream, bushy black hair, and a captivating smile; and, as she mentioned earlier, she's also gay. She has a master's degree in business administration and a bachelor's in criminology—quite a combination, don't you think? I hired her as my PA even before she graduated college and made her my partner before she turned thirty. She's one hell of an asset, and I trust her judgment implicitly.

"It had to start from there and work its way out," she said.

"Who needs those criminology classes when you've got boots in the dirt, right?"

"Certainly seems that way," she said. "But the problem is..." She flicked through the photos as I squinted up at her. "There aren't any notes of other injuries to the bodies."

I stood up quickly and looked down at the screen with her, an image of one of the reports made large on the phone's screen. I scanned what was typed and the scribbled notes, then turned my attention to her.

"There's nothing on any of them, is there?" she asked.

"Not that I recall seeing," I replied. "And, to be honest, I wasn't expecting much."

She nodded. "I know you haven't been sold on the idea of foul play here, Harry, so I tried to keep it to myself, but I was waiting for something to come up. Stab wounds. Bullet wounds. Something that explained what was really going on here, but in everything I looked over, there was nothing besides death by train. It was never questioned, and I have to wonder why?"

I folded my arms and looked down at the gravel, my chin on my chest, not expecting to see an overlooked piece of evidence hidden among the white rocks; but more I was trying to recreate the incidents of that night, a chain of events that would lead to the two dead men ending up on the tracks with the blood pooling under them, instead of on and around the rails. But I couldn't see it. It was an impossibility. Death from the steel wheels would have been instantaneous. But if they'd been wounded, or even dead, and if they'd lay there for any length of time when they were placed as they obviously were, gravity would have caused the blood to pool. And if they were indeed dead when the wheels hit them, that would account for the lack of blood on the rails; just a little spray. So, as Jacque had pointed out, previous injuries seemed to be the only real explanation for what the photos showed. And significant ones, given the amount of blood loss we were seeing.

"So what're you thinking, boss?" Jacque said after a moment.

I looked over at her, my hands on my hips. "A lot," I said. "But we have to start with what we have and work from there." I looked down at my watch. "And we should probably think about heading back."

"Dinner plans?"

"I promised Amanda."

"And that's one woman you don't want to let down," she said, tucking her phone in her pocket.

"True," I said, "but there's no sense in wasting the drive. Let's go back through those files on the way."

"You think I missed something?" she asked, guardedly.

I laughed. She was more than reliable and rarely missed a trick, and we both knew it. But she still tended to get her feathers ruffled when anyone even seemed to imply otherwise.

"Not at all," I replied. "I'm just curious to see what else is NOT in those reports."

She raised an eyebrow. "Meaning?"

"Meaning, I concede. You're right, Jacque. It looks to me as if the investigation was mishandled from the beginning. Whether it was deliberate or accidental, I don't know. But what I do know is those two boys didn't just happen to drink too much one night and end up on the tracks—"

My phone buzzed in my pocket and I pulled it out, glancing at the screen.

"Amanda already?" Jacque asked.

"No." I swiped the screen and started back toward the car, the rocks crunching under my shoes. "Text from Tim. Said he's still hacking away but hasn't found anything significant yet."

"Good," she said, surprising me.

I looked over at her, my eyebrows up.

"Harry Starke being convinced he was mistaken is enough of a bombshell for one day," she said, smiling at me as she stumbled along beside me.

I laughed. "I know I make mistakes," I said. "I just try to put years between them. It doesn't pay well to make mistakes in this business."

"Well," she said and put a hand on my shoulder, "that's why you have us around."

I shook my head, grinning. "Come on, you. Catherine was right. Let's get the hell out of this horrible place."

5

Tuesday, April 12, 6:45am

THE NEXT MORNING, I WAS SITTING AT THE DINING ROOM table, a cup of coffee in front of me, the steam long since vanished from its surface, musing to myself about what we'd learned the previous day. Or, more to the point, what we hadn't learned.

I hadn't slept well, and it was hardly a question of why. I knew why, but I had to wonder for a moment what it was like to be a run-of-the-mill type of guy. You know, an iron worker, accountant, even a fireman. Guys who went to their jobs and then left it behind them when they went home. I'd been in law enforcement all my working life, ever since I graduated from Fairleigh Dickinson back in '97.

In the early days, it hadn't been much of an issue. If I couldn't sleep, I just kept working. It was half the reason I'd become so successful at what I do. I hit the ground running and was relentless. Not that I've slowed down that much over the years, but now, with Amanda and Jade in the picture, I've been trying a lot harder to separate home and work. If it hadn't been for those two, I likely would've spent the night at my desk in the office.

I swirled the tepid coffee around in my mug and took a drink. Maybe the balance was a good thing. My back at least appreciated me not spending fourteen hours in a desk chair.

I shook my head, stood up, walked into the kitchen and went to the coffee machine and refilled my mug, trying to warm what liquid was still inside. It was then that Amanda came into the room, tying the belt of her silky green half-robe as she walked. That color and her blonde hair made for a stunning combination.

"I figured I'd find you here," she said, taking a mug from the cupboard and holding it out to me.

I spoke as I poured. "I figured I'd kept you awake with my tossing and turning most of the night."

"Must be a tough one this time," she said as she pulled out a chair at the table. "Though, if I'm being honest, you were due one."

"What do you mean?" I asked, sitting down beside her.

"You get... antsy when things are too easy for too long."

I laughed. "Well, that's quite the situation to be in. Antsy if the job is easy, insomniac if it's too hard."

"I'm not saying it's too hard," she said. "They're never too hard for Harry Starke. But it's just how you work. When you've got a puzzle, your brain can't shut off until it figures it out. Believe it or not, it's one of the things I like most about you."

I raised my eyebrows. "Just one of the things?"

"Easy there." She grinned. "I like it sometimes. When you sit at the table and stare off into the ether for twenty minutes straight, or when you flop around like a fish out of water all night, maybe not so much then. But hey, 'for better or worse,' right?"

"One of these days, I'll find a flaw in you," I said.

She laughed. "That is one puzzle that shouldn't keep you up all night. And," she said and sipped her coffee, "one I'd rather you didn't spend too much time thinking about. So let's hear about this new one. What's the problem that stole my husband away from a perfectly fine dinner last night and now breakfast this morning?"

I glanced over at the stovetop.

"No." She waved a hand. "I'm not hungry anyway. But I'm curious. Tell me about it."

"I don't know," I said. And it wasn't from any desire to keep things from her. Amanda had been more than valuable to me more than once as a sounding board. As an investigative reporter, now a news anchor, she had a way of approaching problems that was just... different from how we were trained at the academy and what most of my staff had learned from me, Bob Ryan and Heather, though Bob was now long gone, back to the CIA.

No, Amanda's was always a fresh perspective and I'd come to realize that was perhaps the most valuable trait in any investigation. The more someone becomes convinced of a pet theory, the harder it is for that person to let it go, despite what the evidence may say. Amanda had no horse in the race, so she was ready to do the necessary mental gymnastics and call me out when mine were getting too complicated.

"Okay," I said. "It's like this."

I gave her the quickest overview of the situation I could, letting her ask the questions that seemed pertinent to her without introducing too much prejudice from the rest of us one way or the other. I was lingering on the crime scene, the lay-out of the bodies, the blood, when she held up a finger.

"Wait," she said. "Go back to the part about the ME reports."

"What there was of them didn't mention anything about other injuries," I said.

"Right, you said that before. Not the lack of information about injuries specifically, but that it seemed short."

"Short is a generous description," I said. "The examiner could've fit her findings on a playing card and you still could've seen the pips."

"There you go," she said.

"What?"

"What else isn't there? I think you're on the right track with the missing info about the other wounds, but that can't be the only thing you'd expect to find."

I started to speak and then closed my mouth. She'd done it again. Jacque and I had been too focused on what we weren't seeing with regard to the wounds that we'd stopped focusing on anything else. And that anything else was a whole lot of things.

"Keep going," I said. "What are you thinking specifically?"

She smiled. "Oh, I like this part." I watched as she walked over to the coffee machine, sashaying slowly, enjoying the moment.

"Come on, Amanda. No one likes a gloater."

She turned her head and gave me a pouty face. "Let me enjoy my moment."

Having refilled her cup, she sat down again, smoothed the hem of her robe over her thighs and folded her hands on the table in front of her. "All right, all right," she said finally. "I probably shouldn't gloat considering one of you likely already thought of this. But what's the one thing that's missing, Harry? Two young men get so blotto-ed that they pass out on the tracks and don't wake up, not even for a train whistle. Maybe it seems obvious, but you know how those reports have to be. Meticulous. Everything justified. Everything written down. So what's the one thing we don't have proof of? Not the blood, not the injuries. Just the one basic fact of the story so far."

"The tox screen," I said.

"The tox screen." She smiled at me over her coffee mug. "Surely, even if everything else was missing, they'd want something in there to prove the story. Otherwise, you just have two dead bodies and someone else's story about how they probably got there. And if, as you say, there were wounds to the bodies, why weren't they noted on the ME's reports? It seems to me it's a case of either there weren't any such wounds, or there was some kind of cover-up."

It seemed obvious when she pointed it out, but I'd already raced so far down the path I'd forgotten to start with the first step. If I was going to dive into this, I needed to see everything that had happened, or didn't happen, along the way. If it wasn't written down, as they'd told us over and over in training, then it didn't happen.

"You think they left the tox screen out on purpose?" I said.

"Whoa." She held up her hands. "I'm not thinking anything of the sort. At least not yet anyway. I know these guys, Harry. And you do too, though maybe not in the same way. When another investigator comes barreling in, I would imagine the main goal is to get the person out of the way as quickly as possible. But when a reporter shows up, nine times out of ten, people don't see a threat. They see an opportunity."

She'd explained it to me a few times before. Back when she'd worked as a reporter, more often than not, her interviewees saw the chance to turn her questions into a soapbox.

"These guys are overworked," she said. "I know you were on the force too, but Cleveland is a whole different ballgame. They don't have the people they need. They're always rushed. You said yourself there's a fairly new chief with files stacked to the ceiling. Maybe the solution to the missing tox screen is just that somebody didn't have time, put it off until later and just forgot to add it to the file. Or, even more likely, left it lying on his or her desk and it ended up somewhere else by accident. If I were you, that would be where I'd start. Just make a phone call. A *friendly* one." She grinned.

"Maybe," I said, looking down into my mug and trying to play out scenarios as to how that conversation could go.

"All right," she said. "Call Doc Sheddon first. Get some professional backing before you go chasing down dead-ends."

"It's like you read my mind," I said, leaning over to kiss her on the cheek.

"Just remember," she said as I rinsed out my mug in the sink and headed for the door. "A misplaced file could be nothing more than a *misplaced* file. Heaven knows how many places I've found your keys lying around here in the last month."

I patted my pants pocket.

"They're on the end table in the living room," she said, laughing. "Love you."

6

Tuesday, 8:30am

Jacque was at the coffee machine when I walked into the office that morning. I slung my laptop bag over my shoulder and went over to join her, taking a mug from the rack by the sink.

"Any breakthroughs during your sleepless night?" she asked.

I laughed. "Am I that much of an open book to everyone these days?"

"You are," she said. "And you look tired."

"Good morning to you too." I smiled. "And maybe, though I think we're already tripping over our own feet, we need to go back to the beginning and start picking this thing apart as if we know nothing at all."

She held her hands out. "That's not so far from the truth."

"Fair. But from here on out, no assumptions. We verify everything."

"If it's not written down, it didn't happen. Got it," she replied.

"Speaking of..."

"I sent you an email this morning. Every photo I took is in your inbox."

"Perfect," I said. "You guys keep doing what you do best. When Heather and TJ get back, you can bring them up to speed. As for Tim—"

She held up her hand. "Hey, whatever it is that lit a fire under you this morning, go get after it. I can handle this side of things. And if it gets too overwhelming for a poor, delicate flower like me, I do know how to knock on your office door."

I nodded. "Right! Okay! You know where to find me." And I went to my office, coffee in hand, and pushed the door shut behind me with my foot. I had a rough idea of what I wanted to accomplish, but every step in the plan for the day had the potential of spiderwebbing out into uncharted territory, and those were the kinds of distractions I didn't need. They almost always led me to pools of blood instead of tox screens.

I set the coffee down on my desk and took my computer out of the bag, opened it and found the file Jacque had sent. I pulled up the photos, arranged them on the screen as best I could and then called Doc Sheddon.

The man was meticulous, something I needed, and practically married to his job, something I'd come to rely on more than I realized. He was the kind of small, almost cartoonish character that it would be easy to take advantage of, if he hadn't been around as long as he had. The joviality was only one side of his character though; his professionalism was the one trait that, while it was assumed, it took time to realize how deep in his psyche it ran.

Doc Sheddon was the type of guy whose knowledge and opinion I'd take over just about anyone else when it came to his area of expertise. The fact that it was dead bodies was something that set him apart, sure, but it also made him invaluable to people like me. Not to mention the cops and the families he'd been there for along the way.

He picked up on the first ring and had probably already been sitting in his office for an hour by the time I called.

"Harry Starke," he said, a smile evident in his voice. "How have you been?"

"Well enough," I said. "Yourself?"

"Always busy. Can't complain," he replied with a lift in his voice. "To what do I owe the pleasure so early in the morning? I haven't heard you were involved in anything that might also involve me of late."

"I'm branching out," I said, feeling myself relax a little. "I was up in Cleveland yesterday on a case and I have a couple questions for you."

"Ohio or Tennessee?"

"Tennessee," I said. "I'm not ready to branch out quite that far yet."

Doc laughed, almost what one might call a titter. "Well, I'm always happy to help, if I can. What can I do for you today?"

"I have the ME reports," I said, moving the photos to the middle of the screen on my computer as I spoke. "Or at least, that's what they're supposed to be. You wouldn't happen to know a Brenda Polaski, would you?"

"Actually, I do," he said, surprising me. "At least by name. I don't believe I've ever met the woman face-to-face. A phone call here and there, maybe. She filed the paperwork?"

"Well," I said. "Yes and no. I've got a bit of a hodgepodge of things here. Some of it's squared away, while other parts seem to be pretty much lacking. I figured since you're the expert, it would make sense to get your take on it rather than sit here scratching my head. I can email you the files if you'd like."

"I'll do you one better," Sheddon said, surprising me for the second time in so many minutes. "I'll be over in your neighborhood around noon today. How about I grab us some lunch and we'll take a look at it together? Quicker than email after email."

I smiled. It was another thing I always liked about Doc. It's not that I dislike technology as a rule, but when it comes down to it, I'd always rather have a person standing beside me going over things than spend twenty minutes explaining a typo in an email before getting to the point.

"That sounds like a plan," I said. "If you're flying, I'm buying. See you around twelve, then?"

"I'll treat it like a showdown." He laughed. "High noon it is."

I hung up the phone and looked down at my watch. A face-to-face meeting was certainly better than what I'd anticipated, but it also left me with some time to kill. I didn't want to try and talk with Polaski until after my meeting with Doc, so I leaned forward and began flicking through the other images on the screen. I needed to do it slowly, purposefully. And I needed to make some decisions: who was I going to contact first?

I clicked on a file—the initial report—bringing it to the top of the stack. It was as good a place to begin as any. I scanned over the information, looking for anomalies but quickly realized when information was this scant, it wasn't difficult to keep it all in mind. I leaned back in my chair and looked out the window.

Well, I thought, if it worked with Doc, why not keep doing it?

I found the name of the investigating officer, a Sergeant Louise Baker, and pulled up her file. She'd long since left Cleveland, though it didn't appear to be for warmer waters and greener grass. She'd headed northwest to Anchorage, Alaska. Whatever would possess a person to leave the mostly sunny climes of east Tennessee for the frozen north was beyond me, but to each their own, I figured.

I did some quick math in my head. It was going to be early in Alaska, almost too early for anyone to be out of bed unless they had to be. But, at least one person always had to be. I found the number for the police department and made the call.

My call was answered by a chipper young woman. I glanced at my watch. It was still not quite six in the morning there. Either she'd just started her shift or was antsy to get out the door. I introduced myself and, after exchanging an unreasonable amount of pleasantries—then again, what does one really have to talk about in Alaska except the weather?—I got to the point.

"Louise Baker?" the woman said. "Oh, sure, I know Louise."

It's funny the things you notice in people. Regardless of whether she answered the phone in Alaska, the lady had a distinct Minnesota accent. Maybe folks up north like to stay up north. Way up north.

"She's not gonna be in here for a bit, though. If ya like, I can give ya her cell. Might be quicker to track her down that way."

I smiled to myself. They say southern folks are overly friendly, but we certainly don't have a monopoly on it. "Are you sure that's all right?" I said. "I wouldn't want it to come back to haunt you; giving out personal information."

"Oh no, you don't need to worry none about that," she said. "Us law folks gotta stick together now, don't we?"

"That we do," I said, grinning even more as I tried to form a mental picture of just who this voice belonged to.

"You got a pen?" she asked.

I wrote down the number and, after another minute or two, was able to break away from the conversation. My hope being that Louise herself was as forthcoming. Assuming I didn't pull her out of bed.

I glanced again at my watch and figured, why not? If it was a personal line, there was a good chance she turned it off in the evenings anyhow. After any length of time in law enforcement, ringing phones when you're off duty somehow gets in your psyche; your brain always associates it with bad news. And even the chance a phone might ring can wreak havoc on your sleep. I figured I'd leave a voicemail and then move on to the next task.

The phone rang once, then a clear voice announced, "Louise Baker speaking."

"Ms. Baker," I said. "I apologize for calling so early in the morning. I was going to leave a message."

"Ah, well, you got me instead," she said, her voice and accent sounding even more familiar after the unique conversation I'd just had. "Who is this?"

"My name's Harry Starke," I said. "I'm a PI in Chattanooga, and I'm working on something I think you might be able to help me with."

I couldn't be sure, but there seemed to be the slightest pause before she responded. "I haven't been down that way for almost five years," she said, sounding as if she were picking her words carefully. "I'm not sure what I could possibly do for you."

"I understand," I said, trying to relax my tone and make it sound more like a long shot than an interrogation. "I had a couple of fellas come into my office a couple of days ago asking if I'd look into an old case in Cleveland, and I came across your name on the file. Well, it seemed to me it made the most sense to talk with the person who was there rather than wander around in the dark."

There was that pause again, then she said hesitantly, "All right."

This was why I preferred to talk to people face-to-face. If I could see the woman, I'd be able to gather ten times as much information by watching her facial expressions and body language than just the tone of her voice on the other end of a phone call. But, in situations like this one, it was best to just dive right in. "I'm looking into the deaths of Dillon Harper and Brian McDaniel. This was a few years ago now, but—"

"I remember," she said, interrupting me. "There's not much to look into, though. Just a couple of delinquents got themselves drunk and run over by a train. I know it's unprofessional, but good riddance if you want to know the truth. None of that lot was worth the air they breathed."

Her response, the way she spit the words, put me off a bit. I'd been expecting evasion, maybe even feigned confusion, not instant disinterest.

"I see," I said. Now I was the one choosing my words carefully. "But that's not how their brothers see it. It was them who asked me to look into it."

She let out a short laugh. "Jake and Blake? They're nothing but a couple of spare parts. Next thing you know, you're gonna tell me Alan Woodward's ringing your bell. Do yourself a favor, don't waste your time. Those two boys got what they had coming to them, and I won't be a lick surprised if something similar happens to the rest of them."

I grabbed a pen and scribbled down the name. "Alan Woodward. Something similar?"

"Don't act like you haven't seen it before, officer," she said, and I didn't bother to correct her. "Those boys are the dregs of society. Your best bet is to just stay away from them. They're not going to bring you anything but trouble."

I ignored that. "I just want to double-check something," I said, trying to control the pace of the conversation. The more she said, the more vehement she'd become, her words picking up in pace as well as force. "The ME concluded their deaths were accidental. D'you concur?"

The pause this time was longer, as if she was just realizing she'd said more than she ought. "Listen," she said, her words firm again. "I don't work down that way anymore and I'm happy where I'm at. You want to look into it, be my guest, but you're just chasing your tail. I've told you all I know. Those two boys got liquored up and run over. That's all there is to it. Any other looking around you want to do is going to be a waste of time."

I was about to respond when my phone screen lit up. I held it out in front of me. She'd ended the call. Maybe technology wasn't so bad; I'd at least been saved from the thunk of a receiver hitting the cradle.

I couldn't think of the last time I'd had two such disparate conversations in such a short amount of time. From the same PD, no less. It really does depend on who you talk to. I set the phone down on the desktop, aimlessly circling the name I was certain she hadn't meant to give me. For all her advice to leave it well alone, I think Louise Baker had to know she was just prodding me forward more. I might put some time between my next conversation with her, but this was hardly something I could let lie.

On a hunch, I grabbed my phone and dialed another number.

"Harry," Kate said. "Are you finally gonna fill me in on the big secret case, or not? If so, you better make it quick. I'm literally standing outside the conference room."

"Seems like I oughtta make it last an hour or two then." I laughed, knowing we shared a mutual hatred for the tedious bureaucratic sit-downs.

"Can't today," she said. "Tick tock."

"All right," I said. "Here's the short version. A few years back over in Cleveland—"

"Hold that thought," she cut in. I could hear some background noise and a brief moment of chatter as she moved away from wherever she was to wherever she thought might be more suitable. A few seconds later, she came back on, her voice low.

"Listen, I can't talk right now, and I'm not even sure how much I want to get into this, but if you're getting involved with Cleveland, I suggest you proceed with extreme caution."

I felt my brow furrow. This was a side of Kate I'd rarely, if ever, seen. "What do you mean?"

She said something to someone passing by. "Just be careful up there, Harry, is all. I gotta go. Don't do anything stupid."

My cellphone screen lit up again as, for the second time in as many minutes, I was hung up on.

The cheery desk clerk in Anchorage had been a surprise. Louise Baker, even more so. But Kate Gazzara? Hanging up on me was something she never did. And when things piled up this quickly, despite what might have been in my best interests, I wasn't about to slow down. I flipped through the pages of the notebook in front of me, finding the information Jacque had written down during the initial meeting that had started all this, found the number I needed and dialed.

"Talk quick," was the first thing I heard. Apparently, this was the day for it.

"Jacob, it's Harry Starke," I started.

"Aw, yeah, hello. Listen, Mr. Starke, I'm at work right now. I can't really step away. Did you find something?"

"Maybe," I said. "But for brevity's sake, I just want to ask you about a name. Alan Woodward. That ring any bells?"

"Sure, sure." The background noise almost drowned him out. "He used to run with Dillon and Brian. You ask him; he'll tell you he was supposed to be with them that night. And he never gets tired of tellin' that story."

"Do you know where I can find him?"

There was a crash on the other end of the line, followed by a string of curses I would've needed a thesaurus to come up with. "Mr. Starke, I gotta go!" And he hung up.

I tossed the phone on the desk and leaned back in my chair. I was three-for-three on hang-ups. If things were going to continue in that fashion, it was going to take a week to complete a single conversation.

I ran my hands through my hair and looked down at the paper, then up at the screen. Well, if the job was easy, everyone would do it, right?

I grabbed the pen off the desk and got to work.

7

Tuesday, mid-day

BY THE TIME DOC SHEDDON KNOCKED ON MY DOOR, I WAS more than ready to take a break. Granted, a working lunch was hardly a reprieve, but it would at least get me out of my head. I'd made a round of the office about an hour previous, but every member of my staff was hunkered down and the last thing any of them needed was an interruption from me. Heather and TJ had headed off to track down the train engineer on our latest case, making my pickings even more slim. Thankfully, Doc was, as always, right on time.

"I see things haven't become any clearer since our earlier conversation," he said, reaching into a plastic bag and pulling out two foot-long sandwiches.

"Clearer? No," I said as he handed one to me across my desk. "But, we don't do this because it's easy, now do we?" I reached for my wallet, but Doc waved a hand at me.

"You can pay next time," he said. "We can consider it my fee for whatever puzzle you might have."

I smiled. The man was a rare type.

"Well," I said. "I appreciate you taking the time, Doc. I really do."

"Think nothing of it, my boy. All's quiet at Dead End, for the moment, anyway."

My boy? Geez, he's only ten years or so older than me.

The "Dead End" thing was a reference to the road sign he'd found somewhere and had mounted at the back entrance to his forensic center.

"I'm not sure if you're going to like this one or not," I said, laying my sandwich down for a moment. "It may be more of a paper-work question than a full-blown mystery."

He took a bite of his sandwich, careful to keep any stray slivers of lettuce or shreds of cheese on the paper. He chewed thought-fully, swallowed and said, "One might say *The Adventure of the Dancing Men* was paperwork as well."

I laughed. Doc Sheddon did love his Sherlock Holmes. "Fair point," I said. "But, we are currently lacking a code. We actually seem to be lacking most of the paper as well."

Before he'd arrived, I'd printed off the photos Jacque had sent me and arranged them as best I could. I'd stacked them on my desktop, with those I thought he'd find most interesting on top.

"Two young men were killed up in Cleveland a few years back. Story goes they got three sheets to the wind and passed out on the train tracks. After that, it was just a matter of time..."

"I'd say that would require a few more sheets than just three," he said, putting his sandwich to one side. Then he wiped his fingers on a paper napkin, picked up several of the photos and glanced through them.

I watched as he scanned each sheet, setting them in an orderly pile on the edge of the desk as he finished, asking questions as he did so.

Finally, after picking up the last of them, he picked up the whole stack and looked through them again, this time in silence. Finally, he took a deep breath, looked up at me and said, "This... is a prank? Or an actual bona fide puzzle?"

I cocked my head to the side. "How do you mean?"

"This," he replied as he held up the papers. "This can't be the actual report. Where's the rest of it?"

"That's it," I said. "Those came right out of the chief of police's file cabinet. That's all he has. At least, that's all he knows about."

"And you trust the man?"

I had to smile. "I watched as he took the file out of the cabinet and handed it to Jacque. Then he left us to it, in his office, alone. Who does that? Yes, I trust him."

"Hmm." Doc set the photos on the desk and leaned an elbow on the arm of the chair, his chin in his hand. "This is just..." He looked up at the ceiling. "No, it's..." He leaned forward. "Harry, this is embarrassing. Whoever did this, this Brenda Polaski woman, I can't believe she even put her name to it. Something must've gone missing between then and now. I mean, where are the tox screens? Where are the autopsy reports, for goodness' sake? Any Joe off the street could have done better than this."

He looked through the pages again, as if searching for an example, but then gave up in exasperation. "It's absurd that this kind of work would be allowed."

I crumpled my now empty sandwich wrapper, wiped my hands, took a swallow of lukewarm coffee and leaned back in my chair, elbows on the armrests, fingers steepled together in front of me. "You know, Doc," I said thoughtfully. "You took the words right out of my mouth. Who would ever file something like this?"

"It smacks of a cover-up to me," he replied. "There's nothing here. You realize there isn't a single autopsy photo of the bodies? Not one."

I sighed, nodded and said, "About an hour before you arrived, I talked to the lead detective on the case. It was... interesting, to say the least, in that she was less than helpful and highly critical of the two kids and their brothers; dismissive is what she was. But look, this is what I have, all of it. In all my career, I've never run into anything so... anything like this before. So, in your professional opinion, missing documents and all, how d'you think I should handle it? I've every intention of giving Doctor Polaski a ring, but I don't want to go in without someone knowledgeable backing me."

Doc licked his lips, a nervous gesture I'd rarely ever seen from him. He folded the paper back over his sandwich and looked up at me, his normally happy face the epitome of concern, and said, "Harry, I could count on one hand the number of times I've suggested this, so I don't want you to take what I have to say lightly. But in my professional opinion, if you truly want to get to the bottom of this, you're going to have to start over again, from the very beginning."

I looked at him for a moment before I realized what he was implying. Even then, I couldn't be one hundred percent sure. "Meaning?"

"Yes," he said. "It's the only way to be certain. You need a second autopsy. And for that, you'll need to exhume the bodies."

8

Tuesday, 2:15pm

I TOYED WITH MY PHONE, KNOWING FULL WELL THAT I needed to make the call to Brenda Polaski, the medical examiner on my current case, but hesitating, nonetheless. It was the only logical next step and one Doc Sheddon had wholeheartedly supported. But he'd also been able to drop his bombshell of a suggestion and then left me wondering how the hell I was going to pull it off.

To the man's credit, he argued a solid case, and despite my agreeing with him from the start, his reasoning did a lot to bolster my own confidence in the plan. There really was no other way—whether it was pretty or not was irrelevant. But before I could even begin to deal with the hoops I'd have to jump through there, I needed to talk with Brenda Polaski. Maybe something was, as Amanda had said, not missing but misplaced. After talking with Doc, though, I was almost positive that wasn't the case, but I owed the woman at least a conversation. If, by some odd chance, she had the file tucked away some-where, I'd be the first one to thank her. Unfortunately, though, things rarely work out that way.

I dialed the number I had for her and, after several rings, she answered.

"Doctor Polaski."

"Hello, Doctor Polaski," I began, my tone light but professional. "This is Harry Starke. I'm a private investigator in Chattanooga and have a couple of questions regarding an old report of yours. What I have is not complete. I know how things are, and I'm wondering if the rest of it has gotten lost in the shuffle."

"In the shuffle? What do you mean?" I could tell by her tone she was already on guard, but she didn't hold a candle to Louise Baker. At least not yet.

"Well, I was in Cleveland yesterday and Chief Snow provided me with a copy of his file." It was a little white lie, but what the hell. I needed answers.

"It's regarding a pair of deaths of two young men back in 2018. You may remember it. Two young men passed out on the train tracks and—"

"Yes," she said, interrupting me, her tone curt. "I recall it. Horrible thing to happen. That's what drugs and drinking will get you."

"I can't say I disagree," I said, trying to remain neutral. It's always a fine line talking to people when they're on edge. "Your name is on the paperwork as the medical examiner, and I hate to trouble you, but it seems I'm missing several pages from the final report and wondered if they'd gotten filed away somewhere else, perhaps in your office, or—"

"Why would I keep files that belong in the police department?" she asked abruptly. "Are you accusing me of something?"

"No, no, no—" I started to reply, but she kept going.

"I do my job, and I do it to the best of my ability. It's not my responsibility to make things pretty or easy for laymen to understand. I'm a doctor, and I put in a lot of hard work to get where I am!"

I paused for a moment, letting her blow off steam and waiting to see if she'd completed her brief rant.

"That's the reason I'm calling you now," I said. "I respect a person's job and try to give everyone the benefit of the doubt. And yes, I understand you've worked hard to get where you are, and I'm also sure you're a meticulous pathologist and that you filed all the necessary paperwork. What I'm asking, Doctor Polaski, is very simple. And, to put all my cards on the table, I've had my own medical examiner look over your report, and he is of the same mind. What I have here is incomplete. There are no tox screens. There are no photos of the bodies. There are no autopsy reports. That, you must admit, is unusual, to say the least. I don't care how this happened. All I want to know is, do you have any idea where the missing information could be?"

There was a long pause. Long enough that I held the phone out to look at it, almost assuming I'd been hung up on again.

"Doctor Polaski?"

I heard her sigh. "You must think I'm a terrible person, don't you? That I've hidden things or lost things on purpose? I work hard at my job," she repeated, but the anger was gone from her voice. Now she sounded as if she were trying to convince herself instead of me.

"I don't think anything of the sort, ma'am," I said. "I promise you that. All I do think, all I can think, is that I'm missing some important information and that it must have somehow gotten misplaced. The brothers of the two boys came to me looking for answers, and I'm doing what I can to provide them. I'm sure you can understand that, can't you? Folks want to know what happened to their kin."

It felt a little heavy-handed, a little too "down home on the farm," but part of talking to people is knowing how to say what you want in a way that will matter to them.

"I suppose," she started. "No. I don't suppose." She sighed. "You're right, Mr. Starke. It's only fair. It's what I should've done in the first place."

"I appreciate it," I said, then, just for good measure, tacked on, "We all do."

"I'll come clean," she said, "but not now. I need to... Well, there are some things I need to put in order. Are you free tomorrow?"

"I am," I said, already scrambling for a way to keep this immediate. "But I really don't mean to inconvenience you. We're on the phone already. You could talk to me now and email the missing paperwork."

"No, it will be easier this way," she said. "Come by the office tomorrow morning. Eight sharp. I'll meet you then, and we can get this mess straightened out."

I started to respond and then, despite the situation, almost smiled. She'd hung up. I shook my head and grabbed my mug from the desk. I was batting four-for-four. It was probably too late in the day for coffee, but I could at least go wash the cup out. Anything to get out from behind the desk—and away from the phone—for a few minutes.

I needed a breather.

9

Tuesday afternoon, late

THE REST OF THE AFTERNOON DRAGGED ON.

There's little in the world that gets under my skin like a post-poned meeting, especially a meeting that's shrouded in some kind of mystery. Maybe it's the still-lingering remnants of the cop in me, or maybe it's just part of trying to be a stand-up person, but when the good guys start to turn, I run out of patience very quickly.

Around four-thirty that afternoon, I figured I'd made it far enough into the day to throw in the towel. Maybe I needed Amanda's perspective again, or maybe I just needed the distraction my family provides. Either way, I gathered up my things and headed for the door.

As luck would have it, Heather and TJ were just returning from tracking down the train engineer who'd had the misfortune to run over our two victims, and what little hope I'd had of ending the day on a high evaporated when I saw the looks on their faces. It wasn't disappointment exactly, but maybe something more akin to doubt or confusion.

"Come on back," I said, turning and walking back down the hall to the conference room. I figured it was the best place to find out what the next roadblock in the case was going to be.

I hooked my computer bag over the back of a chair, settled into my chair and said, "Well, judging by your expressions, this wasn't the easiest of days," I said when they'd sat down. "May as well just lay it on me."

The pair exchanged a glance, and then TJ held out his hand in a "go right ahead" gesture. He was by far the quietest member of the team—still is—and that includes Tim disappearing for days on end to his little command center of an office.

"Well," Heather said, leaning back in her chair and crossing one leg over the other. "The good news is, we were able to track down Mark Johnson. He hasn't strayed far from Cleveland and he was more than happy to talk with us."

"Which is also the bad news," TJ muttered.

I looked at Heather, my eyebrows raised.

"Did you ever know a guy that shot the winning basket in a high school game?" she said. "Or like... oh, I don't know, saw a celebrity out on the street?"

"Sure," I said, frowning.

"That's kind of how this was," she said, mulling over her words. "It felt like this was the only major thing that's ever happened in this guy's life, and he sort of can't get enough of talking about it."

I thought for a moment. "Well, in his defense, I've never run over one person, let alone two, with a railroad locomotive."

"Right," she said. "But it was just... I don't know, Harry. Maybe, after a while, you get used to something like that, but he was just really *into* telling us about it."

"Like you think he was involved? Bragging maybe?"

"No," TJ interjected. "Just a freak."

Heather looked at him for a moment and then shrugged. "I guess that's not entirely inaccurate."

"All right," I said. "Let's hear it."

"If you want the whole vivid tale in all its gory detail, you'll have to track down Mr. Johnson yourself," she said. "But here's the gist. They were rolling in like usual. Johnson says he was 'looking down,' working on something, attending to dials, what have you, when the conductor hollered out that there were men on the tracks. Johnson says he couldn't believe it, seeing as how they weren't near any intersections, 'where you almost expect to hit somebody at some point.' But he looked up, and sure enough, there were two people lying on the tracks."

"Did he say anything about that? How they appeared? Movement? Positioning?"

"Oh, he certainly did," Heather said, almost laughing. "Too much really. Some of it did seem downright strange, though. He said the way the bodies were lying was what initially confused him. Stretched out." She held her hands up over her head. "Arms this way and legs dead straight, no pun intended, 'Like they were doing a pencil dive,' he said."

I nodded.

"He also said that they were not moving and, even after the conductor laid on the horn several times, they didn't move.

'Didn't even open their eyes.' Granted, I'm no train engineer, so I don't know what his position would've been like, but I had to wonder about that last part. There was no way he could have seen their eyes until they were right on top of them."

TJ sighed. Apparently, this was something they'd talked over, and apparently more than once, on the drive back.

"Whatever the case may be," Heather continued, "when the train hit them, it effectively severed anything on the tracks. I won't go into quite so much detail as he did, but suffice it to say there was a lot of mess, what with the cutting, dragging, and so on. Apparently, it took the locomotive several hundred yards to stop. They weren't going very fast, so he said."

I shook my head, not necessarily because of the gory details, but more because if Doc Sheddon and I followed through on his plan, we might have more trouble on our hands than we realized. A decomposed body was trouble enough on its own, and that's when all the parts were where they should be.

Before I could say anything else, there was a knock on the door frame and Jacque poked her head in. "Team meeting without your star player? Shame on you."

I gestured toward a chair. "Come on in. These two were just giving me all the details you need for a really bloody nightmare."

"Sounds like you fared better than I did," Jacque said, pulling out a chair and sitting down.

"Couldn't find the train conductor, Bobby Wallace?" I asked.

"Oh, I found him, but going looking was kind of pointless. The guy could've sent everything he had to say in a text message. And a pretty darn short one at that."

"How do you mean?" Heather asked. "Our guy just about didn't want to let us leave."

"Lucky you," Jacque said.

"Eh..." Heather held her hands out, palms up.

"We can get to that later on, then," Jacque said. "My bit will take about ten seconds. I found Wallace, who's retired now. He said he got out not long after the incident, which is no major surprise really. I mean, who would want to keep running trains after something like that?"

I exchanged a glance with Heather.

"Anyway," Jacque continued, "he said he's been doing his best to put the past behind him and get on with his life. He didn't really want to go over it again. Said he'd given his statement already. Same old song and dance we hear all the time."

"That's it?" I asked.

"Almost," she said. "Just before he closed the door on me, I heard him mutter one thing. I don't even know if the old guy knows he said it aloud or not, but it certainly won't make me want to leave him in peace."

"Which was?"

"'Gotta get the hell out before it catches up with me.'"

"Well, that's one way to make sure every interested party stays interested," Heather said.

I looked over at TJ, who was apparently uninterested in the remark. If anyone had experience with trauma, death, and violence, TJ's experiences in Vietnam would've put them to shame. He also would've been the first to relate to any indication of a haunted past. But, as usual, the man was unreadable. You could tell him Jesus Himself had appeared outside of Walmart on Gunbarrel, and he'd be as apt to respond with "How 'bout that?" or nothing at all.

Jacque started to say something else, then glanced over at the door. Tim, passing by the conference room and apparently having no idea whether it was still standard working hours or not, popped his head in, seemingly surprised to see us there.

"Meeting, huh?" he said, pushing his glasses up. He looked every bit his rag-tag self, shirt half-tucked in, hair askew, and that look in his eye that said his mind was too busy thinking to get too involved with the real world. "Guess I'll throw in my two cents." He leaned against the door frame, hands in his pockets. "Cent one: I'm still looking. Cent two: I'll let you know when I find something worth talking about." He glanced around the room. "You guys have anything new I should know?"

When no one immediately offered any news, he just shrugged and said, "Okeydoke," and melted back into the hallway.

"Kid needs a hobby," TJ said.

"The kid needs something to focus on," I countered. "Right now his list is too long. You know he could find an encyclopedia's worth of information on any one name we might give him. But without a specific target, he's just bouncing around from idea to idea. He knows more about rabbit holes than Peter Cottontail, and that's a fact."

I took my canary yellow notepad from my computer bag and turned it to the first set of notes I'd made. "Here are all the names we have involved up to this point." I read through them, putting marks next to the people we'd spoken with and connecting information where pertinent. "If we're going to keep moving forward, we're just going to have to slug it out, I'm afraid. As far as I'm concerned, the big two we haven't touched base with so far are Alan Woodward and Richard Wickam.

"Now Jacob Harper, that's Dillon's brother, said Woodward used to run around with our two victims and, apparently, can't get over the fact that he was supposed to be with them that night but, for whatever reason, wasn't. I'd like for us to track him down..."

A "clink" came from somewhere out in the hall.

I looked up as Tim poked his head back in. "I heard that. I was just heading back to the den," he said, referring to his office. "Woodward's in jail. Oughtta be easy enough to track him down. I'll do it now."

Before I could say thanks, Tim had wandered off again.

"All right," I said. "Well, that's step one. We talk to Woodward. Anybody fancy a visit to the icebox?"

"We'll go," Heather said, looking over at TJ, who simply nodded.

"All right," I said, turning to Jacque. "That leaves Wickam for you and me. We're gonna load up on these interviews tomorrow and try to get as much done as we can."

"Who else is on the roster?" Jacque asked.

"Well," I said, "this is going to be big, and I'm not sure how it will go over. I need to talk to the brothers and get their permission to exhume the bodies."

"You're kidding?" Jacque said, her mouth agape.

"Nope. I talked to Doc about the case. He maintains it's the only way to get a definitive answer about what happened to the victims."

"In the meantime, though, we need to talk to Richard Wickam. He was the DA at the time. His name's all over our reports. I'd like to track down the parents of these boys and see if they have anything to say as well. And then there's one other thing."

I filled the room in on my conversation with Brenda Polaski and her mysterious appointment the following morning.

"I spoke too soon," Heather said. "I always miss out on the cloak and dagger stuff."

I rubbed the back of my neck, the hint of a headache coming on, though whether it was from the day behind me or the one ahead, I couldn't be sure.

"For all we know, she may bail," I said, "which is half the reason I want to get the rest of the Cleveland folks taken care of if we can. No need to waste a trip. That work for you?" I looked at Jacque.

"I'll be here, bright-eyed and bushy-haired." She put a hand up to the mass of thick curls and smiled.

I nodded. "Good. I don't know about the rest of you, but I'm going to call it a day. We'll meet back here tomorrow afternoon sometime. Hopefully, by then, Tim won't need to spend the rest of his week trying to link any of our guys to the JFK assassination."

10

Tuesday, evening

I SPENT MOST OF THE REST OF MY EVENING ATTENDING TO my fatherly duties, though duty is probably not the right word to use to refer to the time I spend with my family.

Maybe I'm biased, having seen so many unhealthy relationships, deadbeat dads and broken homes, but the time I get with Jade and Amanda is something I value above all else. The fact that I try to use it as a distraction at times as well does, perhaps, sound a little ingenuous, but it keeps me grounded. It reminds me why I do what I do. And it's not just to put food on the table, but to make sure these two ladies live in a world that's at least a little bit safer every day.

As hard as I try though, I can't always put everything out of my mind,;and as we were putting Jade to bed, Amanda gave me that look that said I hadn't succeeded quite as well as I'd hoped. With the little one tucked in, the night lamp on, a noise machine running in the background, the door open a crack, and the monitor on, we slipped back down the stairs to the living room. I sat down on the couch, stretching my legs out onto the coffee table with Amanda curled up next to me.

"Things didn't go as well as you hoped today, I take it," she said, looking up at me.

"Not so much," I replied. "I'm sorry, I don't mean to bring it home. You know that but..." I held out my hands.

"I know," she said, snuggling up under my arm. "I think that's the one thing I'd change for you if I could. I'd give you the ability to turn it off."

We sat for just the briefest of moments before she spoke up again. "Actually, no. I wouldn't change anything at all. The way you think, the way you hunt things down, that's who you are. If it means you're a little distracted sometimes, so be it. At least I know it's because you're trying to do something good and not because you're out chasing girls."

I laughed. "That's one way to put it in perspective, I suppose."

"I'm a realist; what can I say? So let's hear it. I don't know if I'll be able to help, but you know what they say: two heads are better than one, right?"

I turned my head to look down at her uptilted face. Her eyes were glistening. I kissed her forehead, then said, "I'm not even sure where to begin."

"Sure you do," she said. "Like we said this morning. You've gotta start at the beginning and we'll go from there. Last I heard, you were trying to track down Doc Sheddon and an ME who may or may not have any idea what she's doing. That's as good a place to go from as any."

I shook my head and smiled a little smile. "I feel I should probably tell you that this is one of those cases that have both a PG and an R rating, so which version are you in the mood for?"

"Oh. All the gory details, of course." She laughed.

"This one's a little gorier than usual," I said and then gave her the run-down of my discussion with Doc Sheddon, saving the exhumation for last.

"Wow," she said. "That's not something you hear every day."

"No," I agreed. "I try to avoid digging up bodies, if I can."

She thought for a moment and then shifted her shoulders to look up at me. "Did Doc say, like... what to expect? I mean, it's been a few years since they were buried. Is this a box of bones you're wanting to bring up, or will it still be... wet?"

I laughed. "You really do have quite the way with words."

"Hey." She smacked my chest playfully. "I thought that was about as nicely as I could put it."

I reached down and took her hand in mine, playing with her fingers. "To be fair, Doc didn't say anything about it at all. And depending on how things go tomorrow, there may be a whole new plan of attack."

"You found the tox screen?"

"Not quite. Not yet." I sighed. "Not sure. I found the woman who may or may not have made one. She was less than pleased to hear from me, to be sure, but by the time we got off the phone, she'd set up a meeting at her office tomorrow morning. Eight o'clock sharp, so it'll be an early morning for me."

"We have a three-year-old, Harry. When don't we have early mornings?"

"Fair enough. I guess when I quit the force and started out on this wild ride, I didn't give much thought to life outside the job. I was on my own. I could work the hours I wanted to, needed to. If I slept at the office or in the car during a tail, it didn't make a whole lot of difference to anyone. Now I keep thinking things like, 'this trip to Cleveland needs to be over and done with by four so I can get on the road.'"

Amanda sat back and looked at me, faux shock on her face. "Are you... turning into a responsible adult, Harry Starke?"

"Horrifying, isn't it?"

She laughed. "Nah. Kind of a relief really. I was starting to wonder if I'd lost my touch." She leaned up and kissed the side of my neck.

"I think that's the last thing you need to worry about. If there's any woman on earth who can stop me from thinking about decomposed bodies, it's you, my dear."

"Gee, thanks." She stood up and stretched, the little pajama tank top lifting to reveal her flat stomach.

"Well, now, that's a real good start," I said.

She rolled her eyes. "Weren't you just saying you have an early morning tomorrow?"

"True, but who wants to be a responsible adult all the time?" I stood up and put my arms around her waist, kissing her forehead and her lips. "Besides, I've got the rest of my life to be old. Right now, it's all guns, cars, and dames."

She laughed against my chest. "Humphrey Bogart, you aren't."

"No? More of a Dirty Harry?"

"Just Harry Starke. That's all I need."

It was another sleepless night. As I lay in bed, my hands linked behind my neck, staring up into the dark reaches of the ceiling, I was thinking about what Amanda had said and the small amount of information we'd been lucky enough to find so far. Sometimes, when you're younger, you just assume you'll grow up, find a job, start a family and live a normal life. I'd done most of those things, not necessarily in that order or through the accepted procedures, granted, but I was where I wanted to be.

I spent every day of my life working on cases that strayed from the regular pattern. I didn't know the people in Cleveland from Adam, not even Chief Snow if truth be told; but the odds are, at some point, they too had gained all those things for themselves. It's the regular pattern of life, right? No one thinks they're going to end up in a case file. A partially completed one, at that.

I looked at Amanda, sleeping on her side, the red light from the baby monitor glowing on the bedside table behind her. I was a lucky man. My mother had left me a more than tidy sum. My business was booming. Sure, I wasn't going to go out and buy the Titans franchise tomorrow, but I was never going to want for money, no matter what might happen in the future. I could send Jade to whatever college she wanted. I could take care of my girls. What more can a man really hope for?

Maybe Amanda had a point. Harry Starke could be enough.

I adjusted the pillow under my head and looked up at the ceiling. I was enough. But I could also be more than enough. And that's what Brenda Polaski would soon find out.

11

Wednesday, 5am

I WAS UP EARLY THE NEXT MORNING, EARLIER THAN I HAD planned, even for the day ahead of me. Positive anxiety, perhaps? Whatever it was, I knew the last thing Amanda needed was me stomping around the house while she and Jade tried to sneak in a few more winks. Instead, I laced up my shoes and went out for a run. Four miles and twenty-five minutes later, I was feeling at least a little more clear-headed, if not any less amped for the day.

I couldn't put a finger on it exactly, but I had one of my weird feelings. Kate says I have some kind of second sight, and, bless her, Amanda agrees. It doesn't happen that often, but when it does, I take notice. I had a feeling that something was off. Polaski had done little to build up my faith in her as a key component in the case. I was still fifty-fifty on whether she'd even be at the meeting she had so adamantly arranged. But with the full team heading out, surely something was going to come from it. And I was right, both times.

I took a quick shower when I got back, stepping out of the steam just as the first sounds started coming through the baby monitor. Jade was a decent sleeper and, more importantly, a pretty happy kid, and she was already talking pretty well.

"Mamma?"

I smiled. I knew Amanda was on it, so I continued with my daily routine.

By the time I was dressed, ready to go, and on my way downstairs to the kitchen, I could hear Maria, our nanny and bodyguard, making breakfast. I told her good morning, grabbed a cup of dark Italian roast, ate a few bites of breakfast, and lingered for a few minutes with my wife and daughter before the clock in the kitchen told me I was pushing my luck.

I shook my head, knowing I was going to have to fight the traffic to get to Cleveland in time, and having to call in at the office early wasn't going to help me one way or the other. I kissed my wife and daughter, said goodbye to Maria, and hopped in the car to battle the morning rush hour.

Despite the traffic, I rolled into the office with about thirty minutes to spare before Jacque was due to show up. I grabbed a cup of coffee, set my things in my office, and headed down the main hall to Tim's bunker to see if he'd made any progress.

There was no guarantee he'd be there, of course, but after his brief appearance at our late meeting yesterday, I had a pretty good feeling the kid had pulled another all-nighter. Nine times out of ten, he assumed everyone kept the same schedule he did, and I would've received a text, email, and missed call from him at whatever time he'd made a major breakthrough. But it never hurt to stop in and check. Who knows what you'll find on the internet? According to Tim, at least, it's anything.

The door was open about halfway, another sign Tim hadn't bothered to go home. During office hours, when he was focused on a case, the door would be shut and locked, and you could knock till your knuckles broke without a response. Noise-canceling headphones, of course. When he was wandering the halls by himself at midnight, however, he tended to forget this little precaution.

I leaned into the darkened room and waved a hand, catching his eye over one of the four monitors he had arranged in what we have all come to know as the Command Center.

"Hey," he said, his voice and eyes bright, despite the disheveled appearance of his clothes and immediate vicinity. "Forget something?"

"No." I smiled. "Back again. It's a new day, Tim. Regardless of what your shirt is telling you."

He looked down for a moment as if looking for the message written on his shirt. Then he looked back up at me. "Eh." He shrugged. "Who am I trying to impress?"

"You know my answer to that would be 'the clients.'"

"Yeah, but that's why you guys put me in the posh corner office. This posh, *back* corner office. Don't wanna scare away the bunnies."

"Something like that." I laughed. "What's the news? Anything to show for your marathon so far?"

He swiveled in his chair, moving legal pads, printouts, a handful of mugs, and a stack of binders to various positions that only he would ever remember. After a minute, he looked up at me. "Conference room?"

"That might be easier."

"Great. Give me two minutes."

When he walked into the room, he had a load of files under one arm and a rolled-up sheet of paper that could be anything from blueprints to a blown-up version of a postage stamp. The kid got results, and that was all I was concerned about. How he went about it was his concern. I'd learned long ago to surround myself with the right people and then set them loose.

"This one comes with illustrations?" I asked.

"A map." He set down the folders and unrolled the paper in front of me.

I sat my mug down on one corner and looked at what he'd found. "Property map?"

"Exactly," he said. "I know I've been kind of lagging on this one, but the fact is, it's not so much that there isn't a trail to follow as that there are so many trails, and I can't figure out which ones are important and which ones are coincidences."

"Nothing glaring in the two boys' history jumped out at you?"

He shrugged. "I mean, it's Cleveland. You know how small towns are. If something big happens, you're likely to hear about it. If someone makes it big, they don't tend to stay. It's nothing against the town, just sort of how life in a small town works."

I smiled, wondering what other assumptions he'd made about how life works from his secret hideout in the back corner of the building, safely insulated from the very life he was assessing.

"Fair enough," I said. "So we've got two pretty average guys whose claim to fame is the statistically un-average way they died. I can see how that might throw a few monkey wrenches into your world."

"Exactly. So I thought, why not try and get a bigger picture of what's going on?" He grinned. "Get it?"

I shook my head. "I get it, Tim. What am I seeing here?"

"This," he said and pointed victoriously to the printout, "is a map of what I like to call the Harper Happy Hunting Ground."

"As in Dillon," I said, a statement more than a question.

"As in Dillon, Jake, and Dill Harper, to be exact."

"Dill?"

"The father," he said. "The land is technically in his name, but you don't have a swath of land like this and do nothing with it. My guess is more than one bonfire has burned away the night on these acres."

"All right..."

"But look." He pointed along the right side of the map. "See this here? Where the property line ends?"

I leaned down, looking closer. "I'll be. Well, I suppose that answers the question about why the boys were in the rail yard. They walked to it."

"Exactly," Tim said. "Even one step off their property in this direction and they were immediately on the railroad property."

"Okay," I said. "So, what are you telling me? You think they got drunk in the woods one night, wandered off the property, and just picked the worst place to lay down and catch some z's?"

"Your guess is as good as mine there," he said. "It's hard to Google possibilities like that. What I can do, though, what I did do," he continued as he sorted through his manila folders, "was look through some of the other crimes reported in the area around the time the boys were killed." He spread the sheets out across the map so I could see each of the brief histories.

"Any jump out at you?"

"Well..." he said thoughtfully. "I thought maybe the analysis was best left up to the team. I'm more of a hunter-gatherer type."

I laughed. "So that's your role, is it?"

He shrugged. "It works for now. And maybe I don't have a solid theory, but look at some of these." He moved beside me at the table, pointing at each case as he gave me a quick summary.

"Brandon Young. Dies of a drug overdose in June of 2019."

"That's eight months after our case," I pointed out.

"Right, but listen. He dies at home and, according to his wife, he was a dealer, not a user."

I thought about it for a moment. "Could be they were both users and she just didn't want to get brought in for it."

"If he's dealing, there are bound to be drugs in the home. And you know as well as anybody, the first thing they'd do is a tox screen on him and her both."

I snorted. "You'd think that anyway. But all right, so we have a guy who doesn't use drugs dying from a drug overdose in a town where, if we're being honest, there doesn't seem to be much else to do. I don't know if this one is front-page stuff, Tim."

"Just bear with me." He moved the papers aside and pointed to the next file. "Cole Young. I don't know if he was associated with our boys, but the name seems significant."

"You didn't check?"

"I didn't realize you were coming in early," he said. "We can assume yes or no right now. It doesn't really matter. What does matter is he's been locked up for a while now on charges of... can you guess?"

"Distribution?" I asked.

"Bingo. There's Richard Alderman; he's from the same neighborhood. Done time twice for possession in his twenty years of life. Misty Thayer, the rare female dealer. Carter Blackman, possession. His cousin Gregory Blackman, marinating upstate currently after a lab was found on his property. Greg Sneed went missing a month after our victims turned up. His mother filed the report on him." He looked down at the papers on the table. "And that's just what I pulled up this morning."

"Interesting." I let my eyes wander over the sheets, some with mugshots, some barely half a page. "This one," I said, pointing to Greg Sneed. "I want to know more about this guy."

Tim looked down. "Sneed?" He crossed his arms and chewed his lip. "You're sure?"

I cocked my head to the side and looked at him. "Did I miss something?"

"I dunno." He shrugged. "I mean, I feel like we have two guys who die with illegal substances in their systems, I hand you a pile of drug-related cases from the same area, and you pick the one person who's just as likely to have run off."

"True," I said. "Maybe I like the outliers. Call it a hunch. Whatever makes you happy. The point is, you can throw a dart at a map and come up with plenty of drug cases. I want to know why this guy's is in the pile."

"I can tell you that," Tim said. "He's in the pile because it was one of the first ones I came across. If I'd had more time to vet them, I probably wouldn't have included him at all. Other than being from the same town, he's not really related to the rest."

"Well," I said as I stood up from the table, "he made it this far. Let's give him a chance."

"And the rest of them?"

"I like what you're doing here, Tim," I said. "Keep it up. Just put this Sneed fellow at the top of the list. I have a feeling you're onto something. I just don't have the slightest idea what it is yet."

The electronic chime on the front door dinged.

"I imagine that's Jacque," I said. "I gotta go. We're heading up to Cleveland this morning, so if anything pressing comes up, you know how to reach me."

"You got it," he said, gathering up his papers as I rolled the map for him. "I'll tell the others then."

"The others are going to be out of the office today as well, at least for part of it anyway. You, Jennifer, and Mary are holding down the fort, so keep an eye on them if you're up for it."

"Up for it? What's that mean?"

"It means you haven't slept in about forty-eight hours. That's a full week's work plus overtime. If you need to crash, head home."

He gave me one of his grins that always felt equal parts sarcastic and excited. "Crash? Are you kidding me? I've got to find out what happened to Greg Sneed. That guy could be anywhere."

12

_____

Wednesday, 8am

It was fifteen till eight when I eased onto Exit 25 off I-75, took a left and headed downtown.

"That might be a record, Jacque," I said as I made the turn onto 25th.

She turned to look at me. "What?"

"I don't think you said a word on the entire drive."

"Ooh." She gave me an ornery look. "The chatty black girl, huh? Don't forget, as the boss, you're more than open to discrimination charges."

I laughed. "Right. Well, don't forget, as a detective, I'm expected to make observations. What's on your mind?"

She shook her head. "I don't know. This, I guess?" She gestured around her toward the town. "I was so gung-ho on getting in here and finding out what happened, and now..."

"Don't get down on yourself yet," I said. "This is still fresh, as far as being in front of our eyes goes. With any luck, Doctor Polaski will have some new light to shed." I turned right onto Chambliss Avenue and headed toward the ME's office.

"You really think it's going to be that easy?" she said. "This woman falsifies her reports, hides them, and then when we show up, she suddenly wants to come clean?"

"Honestly," I said. "It wouldn't be the first time I solved a case just by asking someone if they did it. People are unpredictable at times. A lot of them just want to get it off their chest. Guilty conscience."

"You think that's what we've got here?" Jacque looked out the window.

"To be honest, I'm not sure what we have. All I know is that she didn't have to set up this meeting, but she did. When we see what happens next, we'll go from there."

"Maybe she just wanted some excitement."

I laughed. "If she was wanting excitement, wouldn't she go to the beach, or see a movie? Anything besides getting herself wrapped up in a crime investigation?"

"You realize who you're talking to, right?" she asked.

I smiled. "Fair."

As we approached our destination, I heard Jacque take in a sharp breath. But before I could say anything, she said it for me.

"Looks like there's plenty of excitement here today after all."

I pulled into an empty parking space and we stepped out. A police cruiser and an ambulance, both with lights flashing, were parked askew at the entrance to the building. A young woman stood off to one side, leaning, or maybe holding herself up, against a bike rack. An EMT was next to the back door of the ambulance, talking into his shoulder mic. And, almost as if on cue, Chief Snow stepped out of the building's main door, walking over to meet us.

"Harry Starke!" he stated. "Well, I'd like to say this is a surprise, but for some reason, I'm feeling a little underwhelmed," he said, standing in front of us, his thumbs hitched in his belt. "What brings you two back into town so soon?"

I nodded toward the building. "Brenda Polaski did. I'm supposed to meet with her at eight. What's going on in there?"

"You were, were you?" He looked back over his shoulder. "Well, I hate to be the bearer of bad news, but I don't believe she'll be able to keep that appointment. Doctor Polaski died this morning. Heart attack, according to the EMTs."

"There's no way they know that already," Jacque said.

"Well, call it a working theory then. Nothing official, but given the circumstances, that's their best guess."

"And what were the circumstances exactly?" I asked.

"Nothing too extraordinary, if that's what you're getting at," Snow said. "Brenda came in early this morning. The young lady over there," he said and nodded toward the bike rack, "Miss Kitner, has been studying under her. A protege, of sorts, though that's not exactly the word I'm looking for."

"Intern?" Jacque suggested.

"Exactly." Snow pointed a finger at Jacque. "Miss Kitner is the intern. The two of them came in around seven, according to her.

Wanted to get the jump on their work, apparently. Now if you believe what she says—"

I held up a hand. "First, if it's all the same to you, I'd like to hear the story from Miss Kitner in her own words. But, second, is there some reason you don't believe her?"

"Oh." Snow rocked on his heels a bit. "I'm not saying that at all. I guess it's just force of habit. Gotta remember to qualify your statements, you know. 'Allegedly.' Things like that. For all I know about Kitner, which admittedly isn't too terribly much, she seems like a bright girl. Though why anyone would make it their bread and butter to cut up dead bodies is beyond me."

"Everybody's gotta make a living," Jacque said.

"Yeah, yeah, I suppose you're right," Snow replied.

I looked over at the young woman just in time to see her dry heave and spit a string of saliva into the bushes behind the rack. "Is she all right?"

"I reckon I better let you ask her," Snow said. "But if you want my opinion, I'd say there's a difference between seeing a dead body and seeing a body die. That's maybe something she wasn't quite ready for."

"Maybe," I mused, turning back to Jacque. "What do you think?"

"One way to find out," she said.

"I assume you'll be around for a bit?" I said, looking at Snow.

"Part of the job." He smiled.

"All right. Come on, Jacque."

We walked over to the young woman. On the way, I pulled a bill out of my wallet, handed it to Jacque and said, "Run in there and see if there's a soda machine or break room. Get her a water or something."

For once ignoring the chance at a snappy reply, Jacque took the money and walked quickly into the building. With any luck, she might pick up on a few things as well. Despite her looks and demeanor, when she wanted to, Jacque could disappear into the background. Just another lady. And that gave her the perfect opportunity to hear snatches of conversation that might have been kept in if it had been me walking the halls.

"Miss Kitner?" I said.

She looked at me through watery eyes, holding a hand to her mouth as her body jerked and she belched. "Oh gosh." She rubbed her eyes with the back of one hand and waved the air in front of her mouth with the other. "Not the first impression I like to make." She wiped her hands on her smock and, thinking better of it, gave me a slight wave instead of offering to shake hands.

"I'm Harry Starke," I said. "I understand you were with Doctor Polaski this morning?"

She cleared her throat, a hand resting delicately on her stomach. "I was. Listen, if you're with the police, I already talked to the chief." She took a slow, shuttering breath. "It's not that I don't want to talk. I'm just..." She waved a hand, trying to cool her face. "Not in tip-top condition at the moment."

"I understand," I said. "And I'm not with the police. I'm a private investigator. I was supposed to meet with Brenda at eight. I know you're not feeling so hot right now, but can you give me a run-down of what happened? Just an overview." I looked behind her, noting Jacque coming back down the sidewalk with a bottle of water. "To spare you the introduction, the lady is my assistant, Jacque. I sent her to get you some water."

She glanced up at Jacque, took the bottle from her and said, "Thank you." She unscrewed the cap and swished some of the liquid around in her mouth before turning and spitting into the bushes again. "It's a taste you can't get rid of," she said.

"I think we've all been there." I smiled at her. "So, if you don't mind, please run us through what happened this morning."

Miss Kitner cleared her throat and, after another small sip of water, began. "I came in a little before seven. Brenda's been helping me with my practicum, and I wanted to get in as many hands-on hours as I could. She said she had a straightforward exam to do and would let me take the reins as much as possible. Practice makes perfect and all." She coughed into her hand. "Things were going along as usual, nothing particularly out of the ordinary with the body or the circumstances of death. We were maybe half an hour in when she seemed like she was losing her balance, you know? Holding onto the edge of the table, swaying?"

"She wasn't prone to fainting?" Jacque asked.

"No," Kitner said. "She would get light-headed if she didn't eat regularly, but that's not an uncommon thing. No diabetes, at least not that she'd told me about. Plus, one of us usually brings breakfast when we come in early."

She looked down at her hands, the vomit tremors slowly subsiding. "Kind of gruesome, I guess. But..." she said and shrugged. "Anyway, she grabbed onto the table, like I said, and then..." She dropped her hands. "She just collapsed onto the floor. I called 911 immediately. I mean, I know basic stuff, CPR, first aid, but most of the people I work with are... beyond resuscitating." She looked from Jacque to me. "I don't mean to sound cold. It's just... the job."

"You're fine," I said, already wanting to ask questions but knowing I needed to let her finish.

"So, she goes down. I call the ambulance and try to do what I can. I never thought I'd say this, but thank goodness Cleveland is a small town. The EMTs got here in no time. To be honest, from what I understand—from what they said—there's nothing they could've done even if they'd been in the room when it happened. She was gone before she hit the floor."

I took in a breath. It was certainly a strange mix of physical reaction with mental distance, but I couldn't really judge. The walls a person in her kind of job must have to put in place to get through not just days, but years of dissecting people, would have to be imposing; hence Doc Sheddon's gallows humor.

"I'm sorry you had to see that," Jacque said, reaching out to rub the young woman's arm. "It's always hard to see someone die like that."

Kitner looked at her for a moment, almost confused, and then her eyes widened. "Oh! Oh, no. I'm so sorry. I know how this must look." She gestured to herself. "I don't mean to sound heartless, but this," she said and pointed to the bushes, "is unrelated. You have to get used to bodies if you're going to do what we do. The nausea is just... I don't know. Maybe I had some bad fish last night. It smelled funny, but I mean, it's fish."

I was about to begin my list of questions when I had a thought. "You said you usually have breakfast here when you come in early, right?"

"Yes." She looked at me. "Not like a full spread, but you know, bagels, donuts. Something we can just grab on the go."

"Did you bring your own?" I asked.

"No..." she said slowly. "Brenda brought it today. A box of donuts. Why? You can't get food poisoning from donuts." She looked over at Jacque. "Can you?"

"You can get anything from them," I said. "Depending on what someone put in them. I need a minute. Jacque, you stay with Miss Kitner."

It took every ounce of willpower not to run into the building, but for the time being, this wasn't my case. So I stepped away and beckoned Snow. "Inside," I said when he joined me. "Miss Kitner says there's a box of donuts. Find them, bag them, and whatever you do, don't touch them."

He gave me a confused smile that quickly faded to seriousness. "You mean?"

"Damn good chance," I said. "It's not a heart attack. We're very likely looking at a murder."

13

Wednesday, 9:15am

PROVING YET AGAIN THAT A RELIABLE PERSON IS WORTH their weight in gold, Doc Sheddon was out of his office, on the road, and in the ME parking lot in Cleveland within forty-five minutes of my call.

Thankfully, Chief Snow had been startled enough early on to just follow my lead when I suggested calling in an ME from thirty miles away in another county. It was one less thing for him to worry about in a situation that had suddenly and exponentially accelerated.

I stood off to the side as Sheddon talked first to Miss Kitner. Beyond learning her first name was the rather unfortunate "Asabelle," the bits and pieces I could pick up from the conversation at least set me at ease that we wouldn't have two bodies on the scene any time soon. The girl hadn't actually eaten anything yet. She and Polaski had gotten to work right away, and the breakfast had sat untouched for most of the hour before Jacque and I had arrived.

Maybe I was wrong, but after Doc headed into the building, his huge black bag hanging at his side, I had enough time to convince myself I was wrong and right many times over.

It took almost twenty minutes, but when Sheddon came back out, he made a beeline for Jacque and me. We'd done our best to hang back, leaning on the same bike rack Asabelle Kitner had used as a stabilizer not too many minutes earlier.

She herself had opted for a ride to the ER just a few blocks away on Chambliss, on the strongest of urgings by both Doc and myself. Snow assured her he'd be able to find her if need be. So, looking both wearied and concerned, the girl had taken a ride from one of the local cops. Snow, in the meantime, had radioed in for his CSI team.

"Your instincts are proven right once again, Harry," Doc said, setting his bag down on the ground and sticking his hands in his pockets.

"The donuts?" I asked.

"Precisely," he said, rocking on his heels. Not often, but occasionally, I wondered if the Sherlock Holmes stories were a little too much for the Doc. Times like this became more of a mental exercise in problem-solving than a real—and rather dangerous— crime scene. But, who am I to judge? I at least get out of the office occasionally. *And those feelings I had that something was off... I was right, again.*

"So we're looking at murder," Jacque said.

"Indeed we are," Doc replied. "Which is why I wanted to speak with you first. Granted, I'm not a law enforcement expert, but I would assume that this place is going to be a little, hmm... busy once I tell the chief my findings. I thought you'd at least like to know before I'm otherwise occupied."

"We appreciate that," I said. "What exactly are your findings?"

"A classic, really," he said, and I could've sworn he was about to rub his hands together with glee. "Cyanide poisoning."

I shook my head, rubbing the back of my neck. I heard Jacque let out a low sigh.

"That's terrible," she said. "Sounds like a mafia thing, right?"

Doc nodded and said, "Cyanide. It's easy and devastatingly effective. It, along with a number of other toxic substances, are all around you if you know where to look. The only factor that matters is the amount. If I had to guess, you yourself are exposed to it multiple times a day. It's just such a low level it doesn't have quite the impact we're seeing here today."

I saw Jacque raise her eyebrows. "I'm no health-nut, I'll give you that, but cyanide?"

"Oh yes." Doc nodded. "Cigarette smoke contains cyanide, though not enough by far to kill you, am I right? Computers, phones, car tires, car exhaust. The list goes on."

Jacque sighed. "So I'm in the clear."

Doc grinned. "Of course. Unless that is, you've ever eaten spinach, or almonds, or lima beans. Swallowed an accidental cherry pit."

Jacque held up a hand. "I get it."

"Tapioca," he said, unable to resist adding one more. "But as I said, like with so many things, it's the amount that matters. Obviously, we've all probably eaten an almond at some point in our life and lived to tell the tale. What we have here, though, has more in common with cocaine than vitamin C. To get a refined amount like this, someone had to specifically seek it out, and, despite what you may think, it's not actually in rat poison. That's arsenic."

"Great." I looked back across the parking area. A few curious cars on Chambliss were slowing down, but Snow had wisely turned off the flashers on the emergency vehicles, and for whatever reason, if the lights aren't flashing, people are less interested.

"So Polaski eats the donut, eats the cyanide, and she's done for," Jacque said. "And the intern, she just walks out of the room without a hitch?"

"Oh, not entirely," Doc said. "She'll be fine, I'm sure, but it was her that tipped me off to what might be happening. You see, when cyanide enters the body, it attacks the mitochondrial electron transport chain within the cells themselves—"

I held up a hand. "We went to college, but I don't think either of us loved chemistry."

"Fair enough," he said. "Basically, it disrupts your body's ability to convert one thing into another. As many poisons do. What you see in very mild exposure are things like headaches, dizziness, vomiting." He glanced at the bush behind us. "Some people report mood alterations, excitement, confusion. That type of thing. Interestingly, though, and perhaps unsurprisingly, the smell of almonds has been noted in numerous cases."

"I'll keep that in mind," I said. "So Miss Kitner, then, she... what? Inhaled it?"

"That's my working theory," Doc said. "Perhaps touched one of the donuts and had some kind of transdermal exposure, but I find that highly unlikely."

"Gloves," Jacque said.

"Oh." Doc looked surprised. "I suppose you may be right. I just thought, who can pick up a donut without taking a bite?"

"Apparently not Brenda Polaski." I sighed. "Just out of curiosity, after eating it, did she have any chance at all?"

Doc looked down and shook his head. "I like to say there's always a chance, but when it comes to something like this, it would've been more of a miracle. Granted, there are always factors to consider. Weight being one. The amount of cyanide ingested obviously another. But at best, Doctor Polaski had about four minutes between the time she ingested the poison and the time her heart stopped."

"You've got to be kidding me?"

"Not at all," Doc said. "It's not uncommon for death to occur in under a minute."

"One minute?" I blew out a breath, looking over at Jacque. "Geez!"

"Do you have any idea what she was going to speak with you about?" Doc asked.

"No... yes." I looked down at the pitted sidewalk under our feet. "I have theories, but without her, we're up against a brick wall."

"I see." Doc looked over at Chief Snow, who had been talking to several of his officers and had called his name and started toward us. "It looks like the work is about to begin."

"Listen," I said, "before you wander off, do you have any idea where this cyanide could've come from? You said it's not easy to find in this particular form."

"Not easy, no," he said, "at least not for law-abiding folks like you and me. But impossible? Clearly not. I'm afraid young Jacque here may be closer to the truth than she realized. Of course, I'm not saying the mafia was involved here, not by any stretch of the imagination. But as far as murder goes, well, if you're willing to commit a crime like this one, tracking down a substance such as cyanide probably isn't going to cause you to lose too much sleep then, is it?"

I nodded. "All right, Doc. Keep your phone handy. I don't know what I'll need to know, but you usually have the answer."

It was at that point when Snow joined the group, his usually jovial face somber.

"You pass along whatever you needed to pass along?" he asked, looking at Doc Sheddon.

"Just keeping everyone in the loop," Doc said, smiling.

"Right." Snow took off his hat and ran a hand through his thinning hair. "Look, I don't mean to sound ungrateful here. You making the connection like you did not only opened up some avenues for us, but you also very well may have saved somebody's life in the process." He looked back and forth between Jacque and me, then continued, "You two seem like upstanding folks, and your doc here certainly knows his stuff, which is why I figured, if it's all the same to you, I think it's best we downplay your involvement here, for the moment, anyway. I'm not saying we're going to write you out or cover things up, but... well, let's just say it might run a little smoother for all of us if we keep this in-house for the time being. I wouldn't be a bit surprised if the TBI shows up when they get wind of this, and I'm going to have my hands full dealing with them."

I glanced over at Jacque. "Unless you have some reason you want to stay and watch the circus..."

"I'm good," she said.

"All right," I said, looking again at Snow. "But please keep me abreast of any developments. Doctor Polaski wanted to talk to me about something, and I intend to find out what it was."

"Wouldn't happen to be regarding a case you came asking me about now, would it?"

I smiled. "You keep your phone on you, too. I get the feeling all of us may be chatting more than we anticipated until this thing is over with."

Snow nodded. "All right then. I'll be in touch."

As Doc and Snow walked back toward the building, Jacque and I turned toward the car.

"That seem a little off to you?" she asked as we crossed the lot.

"Snow?" I glanced at her, thinking. "Honestly, no. You saw his office when we came down last time. The man's already swamped and now he has this on his hands. He's not running us off, and he's not brushing us under the rug. I think right now he's just trying to put out fires."

She opened the car door and climbed in.

"You sure about that?" she asked as I got behind the wheel.

I started the engine. "One hundred percent? No. But if this is how he thinks he's going to get rid of us, he did an amazingly poor job of it. For now, we'll chalk this one up to small-town hospitality until it looks like something else."

"All right," she said, buckling her belt. "You're the boss. But while we're on the topic, maybe let's avoid you bringing in donuts to the office for a while, shall we?"

"Almonds and spinach it is," I said as I pulled out of the lot onto Chambliss.

14

Wednesday, 11am

"Dill Harper?" Jacque said as I followed the GPS going north some four miles out of Cleveland. "Is that a typo? Like Dale? Dillard?"

"Not a typo," I said as I turned off the asphalt and onto gravel. "Weird name for sure, but Tim pulled up a plot map, and D-i-l-l is how they'd marked it."

"Huh," she said, looking out the window.

"I mean—"

She held up a hand without looking over. "It's a perfectly fine name. Just a unique spelling."

I smiled and turned onto a hard-packed dirt drive, a mailbox with "Harper" hand-painted on its side standing guard. The lane ran back, meandering left and right along the crest of a low hill, trees looming over us, but the grass swaths on either side were pristinely mowed and the line between the trees and yard crisp.

"Not a bad little spot he's got here," she said. "A bit out in the boonies for me, but not bad."

I pulled up into a wide, empty space in front of the ranch-style home. A pair of rocking chairs sat on the concrete porch, bushes running along the front in either direction. The house wasn't immaculate, but it was tidy, well-tended. I turned off the car and took a breath.

"Hey, as long as he's alive," Jacque said, unfastening her belt, "we're doing better than we have so far."

"Don't jinx it," I said, climbing out of the car.

The door was answered by a surprisingly young woman. It took me a moment to notice her shirt was actually a smock, and her shoes, the white sneakers that are apparently issued to every medical aide in the country.

"Hi," I said, introducing myself. "We're hoping to speak with Mr. Harper, if he's available. It won't take long, but we'd like to talk to him about his son."

The young woman looked at Jacque, then at me, raised an eyebrow, and ushered us in.

"I'm Claire," she said, "Mr. Harper's in-home caregiver. I'm not sure if anyone's told you about Dill, but he's... well, he's Dill."

"As in?" Jacque asked.

"As in, he still firmly believes he's twenty-five, for starters."

I cocked my head to the side.

"Not, like, in actuality," Claire said. "I mean, well, you saw the yard when you pulled in. He still does all of that himself, despite my firm recommendations to the contrary. Up with the sun, works himself ragged by about ten, then it's a long day of me pretending to not notice when he dozes off. Which, fair warning, could happen at any time. Just don't let him know you saw. He's adamant he doesn't nap. Says it's for weaklings."

"This sounds like it's going to be a treat," Jacque said with a smile.

Claire stopped us before entering the back den. A television could be heard playing what sounded like daytime preaching. "I don't mean to be rude," she said, looking down at her hands, "but you two are...?"

"Work associates," I said.

"All right." She let out a sigh of what sounded like relief. "That should be fine then. Just... Dill is old school, in just about every way you can think of."

I nodded toward the sound of the TV. "Good old boy?"

"The best old boy, if you ask him. Of course, he'd never say so. It wouldn't be humble of him. But you'll get the idea. What is it you're after exactly?" She tucked her hair behind her ears and chewed her bottom lip. Someone in her profession was surely more than a little familiar with confidentiality, and the question seemed like one she wasn't entirely sure she was allowed to ask.

"Just some questions about his son," I said.

"Jake?"

"No," Jacque said. "Dillon."

"Oh... Well..." She put her hands in the pockets of her skirt. "Don't get your hopes up then."

"Not much of a talker?" I asked.

She laughed. "Depends on the subject." And with that, she stepped into the den, crossing over to a large, brown leather recliner. A four-footed cane stood on one side and all we could see of Dill Harper were his black-socked feet and house shoes.

"Dill," Claire said, raising her voice against the volume of the preacher on TV, "you have some visitors. They want to ask you a few questions about Dillon." After a pause, she reached down. "Dill?"

A startled grumble came from behind the chair. Then, "What's that?"

"Some visitors," Claire repeated. "To ask about Dillon."

"Well, why didn't you say so?" the man asked, his tone an odd kind of irritated that reminded me more of a spoiled child than an elderly man, as if he knew exactly how dependent he was on this young woman, but he would be the last to admit it. "I wasn't asleep, you know."

"Of course not," Claire said, reaching over and finding a remote somewhere. "I think you just didn't hear me over the show. The reverend is really speaking the truth today."

"You're darn right he is," the man said, finally craning his neck around to see who his visitors were. "Well, come on in." He waved a fragile-looking hand at us. "No need to stand there like you done something wrong."

Claire gave us a thin smile that almost seemed to be more of a wish good luck and then stepped away. "I'll just be in the kitchen if you need me," she said, her voice still full and clear.

"Oh, I reckon it'd be about dinner time, ain't it?" the man said. I had to smile. I hadn't heard anyone call lunch dinner since my own grandmother passed.

"Soon," Claire said. "I'll get started on it now."

She slipped past Jacque and me and, unsure of how to handle the seating arrangements, I left a straight-backed chair to Jacque and sat on the edge of a small brick fireplace.

"Mr. Harper." I leaned forward, offering a hand. "My name is Harry Starke. This here is Jacque Hale. We were hoping you could answer a few questions about your son."

"I heard what she said." He looked back and forth between us, his mind clearly still moving adeptly, even if his body had slowed down. "Raven and the dove, you know," he added.

I looked at Jacque, Claire's comment finally clicking with me. "We're work associates," I said. "Miss Hale is my business partner."

He looked at us again, clearly noting my wedding ring and Jacque's lack of one.

"You're walking a thin line, young man," he said. "The Lord wants us to be free of any suspicion."

"I'm actually good friends with his wife," Jacque said, picking up the track of the conversation quickly.

"And Abel was Cain's brother," the man said.

You don't work in the South too terribly long before you start to pick up on certain personality traits. I'm not saying everyone is like this, or everyone isn't, but as a detective, I couldn't help but pick up patterns. And Mr. Harper was showing me every sign of a conversation I needed to get in and out of as quickly as possible, unless I was settled in for a good long sermon on everything I'd already done wrong since stepping across his threshold. And the brick underneath me wasn't nearly comfortable enough for that.

"Indeed he was," I said. "On the topic of brothers, your son Jacob came in and spoke with us a few days ago. He asked us to look into what happened to his brother, Dillon."

Dill gave me a long look. "You think I don't know the names of my own two boys?" He laughed. "You get a few white hairs on you and folks are ready to send you to the dump. You see that lawn when you pulled up? I done every bit of that work myself, and I'll keep doing it till the Lord calls me home. You gotta learn to respect your elders, sonny. That's a commandment, after all."

I looked over at Jacque and her expression said everything I needed to know. She knew when to pick her battles, and she was letting me take the lead on this.

"I couldn't agree with you more," I said. "My own father taught me the same thing."

"Smart man," he said. "Religious?"

I'd fallen into this trap too many times. "Yes, sir," I lied and nodded to the television. "Big fan of this program here, as a matter of fact."

Dill gave me another long look, something I can only imagine growing up under. Whether I had told the truth or not, he seemed determined to figure out something I was lying about. Thankfully, I seemed to pass his test somehow.

"The reverend's a good man," he said. "Speaks the truth. That's with a capital T."

I nodded. "Another truth my dad taught me was to respect a man's time. So, considering the reverend is doing the Lord's work, and you're sitting here studying to follow the path, I don't want to keep you too long."

"That's good," he said. "Almost dinner time and I wasn't expecting company."

I wanted to ask him about opening his home to weary travelers, but something told me the longer I sat there, the wearier I would become. "So about Dillon," I started.

"Bah." The old man waved a hand. "You reap what you sow. You dance with the devil and you smell like smoke. The good Lord gave us the ability to make choices and we gotta live with the consequences of what we choose. Dillon learned that the hard way. Ain't nothing can be done about it now."

"What exactly do you think happened to your son, sir?"

He scoffed. "Exactly what he had coming to him. I raised them boys right, you better believe that. But it ain't a man's job to hold his boy's hand every day of his life. I instructed 'em in the ways of the Lord. You look at Jacob and tell me that ain't so. Like another Cain and Abel their own selves. One chose the righteous path, the other went astray."

"A prodigal son who never came home," I tried.

"Oh, he come back," the old man said. "Aplenty of times. But you know the Prodigal come back repentant. Dillon, he come back when his pockets were empty and he needed more money for alcohol, drugs, and loose women."

I needed to change tactics, find a more solid footing. "We've had some trouble tracking down some of the paperwork regarding Dillon's death," I said. "You wouldn't happen to have any files here, would you?"

The pause was long enough that I almost asked again. In fact, I almost looked at Jacque, but I knew one glance from her would get me dangerously close to laughing at the awkwardness of the situation.

"Dick Wickam," Dill said finally, his voice bursting out as if he'd just come to. "That's the man you want to see."

"He has this information?" I asked, trying to clarify what question Dill might be answering.

"He's the DA, ain't he?"

"That's correct," I said.

"Well, then that's where you go. I ain't got no use for them papers. Dillon's gone. He made his choices. I mourned him. Ain't no need to be bringing it up again. The Lord gives, and the Lord takes away. I reckon he figured it was time to take Dillon away. Ole Dick, he'll tell you the same. A good man, he is. God-fearing. And a close personal friend." He sat back in his chair, a proud smile on his face, no doubt sure we were impressed by his familiarity with local bigwigs.

"I'm sure he is," I said, standing up. "We appreciate your time, and we'll let you get back to your program. If we come across anything regarding your son, we'll be sure to let you know."

The old man mumbled something, but by this point, Jacque was already up and we were making a restrained exit from the room. Claire met us at the corner as the volume on the TV came back up.

"You made it out fairly unscathed," she said, a smile playing at the corner of her mouth.

"Did he..." I started.

Her lips made a tight frown. "Yeah... not really a 'love thy neighbor' type Christian. If it makes you feel any better, Dillon's not the only one who can burn in Hell. I'm invited to at least twice a day."

"Then you truly are a saint," Jacque said, putting a hand on the woman's shoulder.

She shrugged. "Gotta eat."

"McDonald's be hiring, too," Jacque said, her voice taking on a sass I rarely heard from her.

"I make better burgers." Claire grinned. "Can y'all see yourselves out? We've got meds, and I don't think that's something you'll want to stick around for."

I nodded. "Duly noted. Thanks for your time, Claire. And, well, good luck."

"The Lord works in mysterious ways, right?"

I watched as she headed back into the lion's den and then turned toward the front door, Jacque beside me. "I reckon it is about dinner time," I laid on a thick drawl. "Care to get some vittles?"

"Only as your work associate." She laughed quietly. "I don't want to be starting any rumors."

"Deal."

15

———

Wednesday, noon

"What would you like for lunch?" I asked as I drove back into the heart of Cleveland.

"Something light, I think," Jacque replied.

"I don't think we're exactly spoiled for choice," I said as I pulled into the lot at Aubrey's. "This should do it, though. They do a nice salad here, if it's anything like the one in Hixson, that is. That work for you?"

She said it would. And we went inside. It was lunchtime and they were busy, but they were able to find us a booth by the window.

"So what's next?" Jacque asked, flipping the laminated menu pages back and forth. "Do we keep on the track of the parents, or move on to Mister Wickam?"

"You mean Dick?" I replied as I perused the menu.

"Never in my life will I ever call a man that," she said, then paused. "Well, not too often."

I laughed. "For the time being, I say we stick to the plan. Odds are, even if Wickam's free, he won't rearrange his schedule for us. It would give the impression he doesn't have anything better to do. Besides, are you saying you don't want to spend some more time with your elders?"

"Harry," she said, "*you're* my elder, so is Heather, so is TJ. I spend all of my time with my elders."

"Ouch."

The waitress came over and set our drinks down on the table, took our orders quickly and disappeared into the kitchen behind the long bar. I watched her for a moment and was almost ready to make a comment about our previous dining experience when a face caught my eye. A hand waved and, before I knew it, I was scooting over in the booth, making room for our surprise guest.

"How are ya?" Jacob Harper said, sitting down beside me. "Didn't expect to run into you two here."

"We go where the work takes us," I said. "How have things been?"

"Oh." He shrugged his shoulders. "Can't complain I guess. Shouldn't anyway. What about you? Any news?"

"Yes and no," I said. "We're hitting some hurdles with the paperwork at the moment. Our first few attempts to track down a complete file haven't been quite as successful as we'd hoped, but by the time we leave town today, we should have what we're looking for."

"That's good," he said, looking off over the booth, seemingly thinking to himself. "Y'know," he started, then shook his head. "Never mind."

"What is it?" Jacque asked. "Anything you think of might be of help."

"Well," he said, and I was surprised to see he appeared to be blushing a little. "I was going to say my father might have something to say, but, well... he's not an easy man to talk to and... I guess I'm not really sure how to say this, but he likely wouldn't approve of your, uh, situation."

"The dove and the raven?" Jacque asked, a devilish smile on her lips.

"How did you... Oh, no. I'm so sorry," he stuttered, blushing even more.

"Don't you worry about it." Jacque laughed. "I've been called a lot worse."

"How was he?" Jacob looked back and forth between us. "He can be a little bit of a basket case. I mean, I want to say he has his good days and his bad, but if we're being honest..." He held out his hands, palms up.

"He seems like a good old fella who's set in his ways and doesn't mind talking about it," I said, trying to lighten the mood. "You can't throw a rock in this state, or any other, without hitting someone just like him. Nothing for you to worry about."

"He's just always been..." He furrowed his brow. "Heavy-handed about it, I guess you might say. I think I saw through him early enough on that it didn't phase me much. Dillon, though." He shook his head. "Sometimes I think Dillon made it his personal goal in life to rile the old man up."

"Well, if it's any consolation, he's still plenty riled," Jacque said.

"Yeah," Jacob agreed. "I wish I'd known you were going to head out there. I could've gone with you."

"It was honestly fine," I said. "We've both seen worse things than old men watching TV."

"You're sure?" the young man asked again. "He seems like he's worn down, but his words can still do what his fists can't anymore."

"Was he rough on you boys?" Jacque asked.

Jacob shrugged. "Who's to say anymore? I don't think we got it any better or any worse than the rest of the kids around here. But, I dunno. You compare it to some other family in some other town and we may look better, we may look worse. I didn't have any intention to stick around any longer'n I had to, so I got out and haven't really given it much thought. You ask Dad, it was his firm hand and raisin' me on the good path that made me what I am today. To be fair, he may be more right than I like to give him credit for."

"Families are tricky," I said. "Nothing ever works the same way twice, and you can't really compare any two of them you find."

"Ain't that the truth?" he said.

"With a capital T," Jacque added with a laugh. "But, hey, while we've got you around, is there anything else you've thought of that might help us out? Like I said, it doesn't have to be a million-dollar idea, just any old thing. We're in town as it is. Figured we'd talk to as many people as we could."

"Yeah." He rubbed the back of his neck. "See, that's the thing.

I've been thinking about this too and nothing's come to mind." He shrugged. "Did Dad get on you about looking into this?"

I shook my head. "Not in any particular way. Said he'd done his mourning and directed us to DA Wickam if we had any more questions. Why?"

"Ah," Jacob said. "Wickam. That'll be interesting."

"How so? You know him?"

"No." He laughed. "That's exactly why it will be interesting. I'm not a hundred percent sure Dad knows him either. He's told me about them being 'brothers in Christ' and what-not, but I've heard him use that term for everybody from Wickam to the apostle Paul."

"Well, we needed to head that way anyhow," I said. "We'll just tell him your dad says hi and leave it at that. Anybody else you can think of worth us tracking down?"

Jacob thought for a moment and then finally sighed. "Honestly, I can't think of too many. The last few years of Dillon's life, I was off spending my time with the glorious US Marine Corps. The last time I actually saw him was about four months before his death. More than enough time for him to get into and out of all kinds of trouble, knowing him."

"Well, if you think of anything," I said, "don't hesitate to let us know. Might be nothing, might be something. We won't know till we try."

"Y'know, now that you mention it," he said, snapping his fingers. "There was one little thing I noticed. You sayin' it may be nothing is what jogged my mind because that's exactly what I convinced myself of as well."

"Let's hear it," Jacque said.

"My shotgun." Jacob glanced back and forth. "I don't know how they do things in Chattanooga, but it ain't strange to have one here..."

I laughed. "I grew up in Tennessee. No need to be concerned about owning a gun."

"Well, some folks are... antsy about 'em. Think just having one makes you a criminal." He looked at Jacque, who shrugged, showing as much interest in his ownership as if he said he had a ten-speed. "It's all legal and everything, so I'm not worried about that. But, I know Dillon used to take it out turkey hunting with him sometimes. It's just an old twelve-gauge, so I don't know how much success he was planning on having. Those twenties they got now though..."

Perhaps he saw Jacque's eyes glaze over, or, more likely he realized he was burning through his lunch break, so he hurried on. "Well, the point is, you get a better range with a twenty-gauge than a twelve, but I don't reckon either would've made much difference for Dillon. Not exactly ready for the sniper school. But he'd take it out every now and again with his buddies. I never kept good track of the gun itself as one of the two of us always had it, but for the life of me, I can't seem to figure out where he musta put it. It's been a few years now and the thing still hasn't turned up."

Jacque looked at me with eyebrows up, and I could already see her ideas clicking by. "October nineteenth," I said. "The date of his death is smack dab in the fall season, so nothing unusual there."

"Oh," she said.

"Oh," Jacob echoed. "No, I didn't mean he'd taken it out for anything criminal. Just, you asked if there was anything strange, and that's all I've been able to think of. Nobody ever said anything to me about him having a gun. I just figured if one turned up with my name on the registration, I didn't want you to be blindsided."

"We appreciate the heads-up. At this point," I said, "I hate to break it to you, but if it hasn't shown up, it likely isn't going to. But that's exactly the type of info you can pass on to us. You never know what will help."

"No problem," Jacob replied with a shrug. "I made it this long without it. Probably time for a new one anyway." He glanced down at his watch and slapped his hands on the table, and stood up. "Welp, I hate to run off on ya, but I gotta get back to it. I'll be in touch if I think of anything, and I'm always happy to talk if something comes up on your side."

"On that," I said, looking over at Jacque and trying to see if there was a tactful way to broach the subject I wanted to discuss. In passing, during his lunch break was probably the least elegant way to do it, but at this point, I was looking more toward efficiency than anything. "I'm not saying we're going to do this for certain," I continued, looking at Jacob. "But with regard to the death certificates that were filed for your brother and Brian, we've come across some problems. If we get our backs against a wall, what are your thoughts on exhuming the bodies?"

Jacob leaned back, his eyebrows up. "Well..." He looked out one of the large windows beside us, trying to formulate an answer to a question he probably never anticipated being asked. "Well." He sighed, repeating himself and looking down. "Ah hell," he said finally. "In for a penny, in for a pound, right? If you think that's the way to find some answers, then you got my blessing. I trust y'all. It's why I tracked you down in the first place, isn't it?"

I nodded. "I'm not saying it will go that far, but we'll need someone from the family on our side, should it arise. I figured you would be the only one willing to give the go-ahead."

He looked down at me, hands in his pockets. "You got my go-ahead, Mr. Starke. Whatever you need." He checked his watch again. "But I gotta get going myself. Nice to run into you." He looked over at Jacque. "Have a nice day, ma'am."

"You as well," she said, giving him one of her warmest smiles.

After he'd joined up with his work buddies and slipped out the front door, Jacque looked over at me, slapped her hands on the tabletop, and said, "Welp!"

I grinned. "It's a good effort, but I don't think you're a good ole boy yet."

"Too much of the raven in me, I guess." She scooted out of the booth. "What say we go find Eddy McDaniel? Continue the day's adventure?"

I nodded. "Right behind you."

16

Wednesday, 2pm

We were about halfway to the McDaniel address Tim had provided when my cell rang. Seeing it was Heather, I answered it through the car's system.

"You're on the air," I joked. "Tell us you've got some good news."

"Oh," she said and laughed. "Long-time listener, first-time caller. We're headed back from our chat with Alan Woodward. Figured you might want an update."

"Maybe the short version," I said. "We're about to pay a visit to Mister McDaniel." I looked over at Jacque.

"Five minutes," she said. "Also, hi."

"Heyyy," Heather sang out. It was funny sometimes. I had picked my team based on their specific skills and qualifications, not necessarily because I thought they'd be best friends at a company picnic. But Heather and Jacque had taken to each other as naturally as ducks to water.

"The truth is," Heather began, "we don't really know what to think. I'd say the best way to put it is that anything we might have anticipated about Mr. Woodward is out the window. The whole conversation was..." She searched for a word. "Weird."

"Ooh, how so?" Jacque asked, leaning forward in her seat.

Heather laughed. "How about we fill you guys in when you get back? You have an ETA?"

"Not at the moment," I said. "Do what you can, or what you need to, when you get back and then feel free to call it a day. We may be chasing our tails up here for a while longer."

We could hear Heather sigh in disappointment. Whatever had happened must have at least been entertaining, if nothing else. "Fiiiine," she said, putting on a faux-pouty tone. "First thing tomorrow, then."

"Sounds good," I said, noticing Jacque's wind-it-up gesture out of the corner of my eye. "Looks like I've got to cut this short. People to see and all those cliches."

"All right, be safe."

Heather ended the call as I rounded the final corner to the address listed for Edward McDaniel. I stopped the car in front of the house and hesitated for a moment. It's difficult to anticipate what can happen on any given day with this job, as Heather had just pointed out. People have patterns of behavior. My job is to have at least a working set of theories and assumptions to make things go smoother, but it seemed like my own guesswork was a bit off that day.

As much as I didn't like to admit I was surprised by the McDaniel home, I was. It was nice.

"Huh," Jacque said beside me, apparently thinking the same thing as she checked the address once again. "I guess that's what I get for being all judgy," she muttered.

"You're not the only one," I said, turning off the car and stepping out.

I rounded the car and had just reached for the gate in the chain-link fence when Jacque quickly put her hand on mine, staying the action. It was then that I, too, noticed the "Beware of Dog" sign. Experience told me that nine times out of ten, signs like that meant nothing. That they were nothing more than the poor man's theft deterrent. After all, ten dollars for a sign was cheaper than thousands for a security system, and still much cheaper than getting an actual dog. The tenth time, though, was the exception.

Eddy McDaniel's sign wasn't lying, as two pit bulls tore around the corner of the house, barking loudly, eyes red and apparently ready to kill. I noticed that the animals followed a clear dirt path in the grass to the gate, something that should've tipped me off immediately that the sign wasn't just a hoax to keep the gullible at bay. I was just about to have Jacque give the man a call when the front door opened and, in the darkness of the home's interior, we could just make out the form of a man.

I raised a hand and announced who we were and why we were there, and, for a moment, the man hesitated. But then, after a long minute filled with the barking of the dogs, he apparently decided to call them off.

"George, Charlie. Off! Place! Git," he called to the dogs. "Git back in yer house. Now!"

The animals hesitated only for a second or two and then, just as quickly as they had appeared, they ran back off to the back of the house, playfully nipping at one another and wrestling as they went.

"Sorry 'bout that," the man said. "Can't never be too careful these days. Damn kids don't have no respect for nobody."

I looked around the houses nearby. It was no Brentwood, but it certainly wasn't the worst neighborhood I'd seen. In fact, in my humble opinion, Eddy McDaniel himself appeared to be the only element of trouble around, and his house the only one on the block the kids weren't supposed to linger in front of.

He was wearing a pair of well-worn jeans that hung loose on his body. His white tank top was not only cliche, but it was stretched and sagging from his nearly skeletal shoulders. I knew I shouldn't jump to any conclusions, seeing as how I'd just misjudged his home, but between the dogs and the stature, Eddy's appearance screamed drug user to me.

I caught a quick glance from Jacque, making me aware I wasn't the only one with concerns, but as the man gestured us in, we had no choice but to slip through the gate and head up the concrete walk to the front door.

"Watch out for stray needles," Jacque said under her breath as we stepped inside.

"I reckon you're here on accounta my boy," Eddy McDaniel said, moving a pile of clothes, chip bags, and newspapers from the couch to the floor.

"We are," I said. "Apparently word travels quickly."

McDaniel shrugged. "Ain't much else to speak of no more. Bin on me own awhile. Life gets tedious, don't it? Set y'self down."

I had to smile at the use of the old Carson Robison song. And, despite Jacque's comment about needles loud in my ears, I gingerly sat down on the couch cushion, waiting for the tell-tale poke. I watched as she did the same and, a moment later, realized Eddy McDaniel was watching us with a keen eye.

We sat in silence for a long moment until I finally spoke up.

"So, your son, Blake, and his friend Jake asked us to find out what really happened that night?"

"Yeah, him, Blake," he muttered. "I reckon I ain't the first person anybody'd come to with questions about the law, and I also reckon what I'm about to say is the last thing a lawyer'd tell me to, but..." He held out his hands in a tired kind of acceptance of the life around him. "I suppose you folks wouldn't be any good at your job if you weren't already making some assumptions about what you just walked into, so I'll shoot straight with you. I hope ya can do me the favor of not getting too up in arms about it."

I was puzzled by the statement but leaned my elbows on my knees and folded my hands between my legs. "We're just here to talk about Brian," I said.

"Well, for your own peace of mind then," he said, leaning back into his well-worn recliner, "you ain't got to worry about no dirty needles around here. I imagine it didn't take you long to figure out I tend to take medicine a little stronger'n whiskey, but I ain't never hurt nobody and don't intend to. I keep to myself and that's the way I prefer to keep it. Ain't nothing out there for me anymore, one way or the other."

Jacque, perched on the edge of the couch, took the tactful approach. "You know, there are places we can recommend you for treatment if your... medicine is a problem."

The man gave her a tired smile. "More of a solution than a problem, though I reckon that's what most folks say." He sighed. "I'm not gonna hurt myself, or y'all, or anybody else. Just... well, sometimes a fella needs a little something to help keep his head above water. I've figured out how to do that for myself. I don't see any need for it to go beyond that."

"All right," Jacque said, appearing to accept the man as he was. It was one of the strongest aspects of her character and something that made her indispensable in a conversation such as this one.

"We're just here about Brian," I said again. "Anything else you've got going on, we're happy to help you out or point you in the right direction, but we aren't looking to take you in."

The man nodded slowly. "Maybe this is an awful thing for a father to say, but by the time it got to Brian, I don't think I was here enough, emotionally, mentally, or whatever, to be much good to you."

"How do you mean?" Jacque asked.

Eddy nodded to a small, framed picture sitting on the end table next to her. "That's what we once was," he said. "Brian wasn't Blake's only sibling. And I didn't used to live in this hovel on my own. Had me a wife. A daughter. Brian's little sister, that'd be."

"A very nice-looking family," Jacque said.

"They was. We was," he said. "But that don't mean much in the grand scheme of things. That picture was taken in August of 2017. By the time October come 'round the following year, I was the only one left, 'cept for Blake, that is."

"I'm so sorry," Jacque said, her tone sincere. "May I ask what happened?"

"With Brian?" he started. "I reckon you already know. Or at least you got the whats, whens, and hows. I reckon Denise—my wife—and Bethany got a file somewheres as well you could pull up. Short version though, distracted driver out on 75. They was coming back from her mother's place up 'round Athens. I told her a thousand times, take eleven. It ain't that much slower. Damn near runs parallel the entire way. But..." He shrugged. "You know how folks are. Good news was, ambulance boys said they died on the scene." He thought for a moment. "I reckon the most I can do is hope that was the case."

"That's terrible," Jacque said.

"Something nobody should have to go through," Eddy spoke down to his hands. "But it don't mean you just let go of everything. Unfortunately for Brian, that's what I did. Started getting into the drugs after the girls' deaths as a way to cope, I guess. Maybe more it was a way to shut everything out. But when I shut out the hurt, I shut out Brian too. He found his own ways to deal with it, I guess, seeing as how I wasn't there to offer him any guidance. He, uh...well, I reckon he got worn down from dealing with it sooner'n I'd expected."

I glanced over at Jacque and then back to Eddy McDaniel. "You think Brian took his own life?"

The man let out a long, shuddering sigh. "It's the only thing that makes sense, ain't it? I ain't got the foggiest what the Harper boy was doing there, but it doesn't take a rocket scientist to put two and two together with Brian. Boy lost just the same as I did. A mother and a sister. Then," he said and gestured sadly to himself, "for the most part, a father as well."

I nodded and started to speak when I felt Jacque's gaze on me. I glanced over and she shook her head almost imperceptibly. I made a small gesture for her to go ahead.

What she said was brief and to the point, that we were sorry for his loss, that we knew grief and drug counselors if he needed either or both, that we'd be available anytime. Then she stood up, apparently finished with the interview. I can almost always trust my team, so I followed her lead, shook the man's hand, and we were back out in the car within five minutes.

"I take it you didn't see that going anywhere?" I asked as we settled in and buckled our seat belts.

"Did you?" she replied. "That man would've talked all day, but it would've been the same thing over and over. I didn't see any reason to push him farther. He's already drowning in regret and depression. Besides, if he had even the slightest feeling that something else could've happened to Brian, I think he would've grasped at even the smallest of possibilities. At this point, he's accepted that his son's death was his fault. If we're going to talk to him about it, I'd rather it be when we tell him we've solved the case and it wasn't his fault, rather than pouring more salt on his wounds, self-inflicted or not."

I thought about what she said and then nodded my agreement. It made sense. It was one of the gray ethical areas of the job. How far do you push someone for information? How do you decide when you're doing more harm than good? I was looking out the windshield absently when Jacque spoke again, her voice almost a whisper.

"You see that? Between the houses," she added.

I nodded. From where we were parked, the scant walkways between the neighboring homes on McDaniel's street were barely visible. Whoever had designed the neighborhood had efficiency at the forefront of his mind, and while the front yards were spacious, the spaces between the houses were barely wide enough for a man, or a dog, to fit through. Eddy had fenced off one side of his to complete the running space for his guard dogs, but on the other side, the fence ran right up to the edge of the house. A man in a dark hoody was lingering in the empty, shadowy corridor between the homes.

"Neighbor?" Jacque said quietly again, as if the man could hear us.

"One way to find out," I said, opening the car door.

17

Wednesday, 2:45pm

MAYBE JACQUE'S INSTINCT TO WHISPER HAD BEEN CORRECT because no sooner had I stepped out of the car than the man turned and disappeared into the space between the homes.

I jogged down the walk to see which way he went, but by the time I reached the alley space, he was nowhere to be seen. I picked up the pace a little, cutting through the slim breezeway toward the backyards, but it was to no avail. A paved lane ran behind the homes and the backs of the houses on the next block were the only thing to be seen.

Jacque was at my shoulder a second later. "Nothing like options," she said. "He could've gone anywhere. You wanna go one way and I'll take the other?"

I was about to answer when my phone rang. I looked at the screen. "It's Doc," I said, glancing back and forth along the lane.

"No," I answered Jacque. "We'll let it go." The phone continued to vibrate in my hand, urging me to answer it. "Let's focus on the problems we know right now," I said finally, swiping across the screen. "Could've just been a curious neighbor and we've got a full afternoon yet."

I put the phone to my ear, turned, and started walking toward the car. "What's the news, Doc?"

"Just wanted to keep you abreast of the situation," he replied. "I have the lab result. It confirmed what we already knew. Massive dose of cyanide. Well, and donut glaze. It was a sweet little trick, using the sugar to cover up the taste."

"Anything else?" I asked.

"Not at the moment," Doc said, "but I thought the fact that our murderer is using cyanide in the most unassuming of ways might be of interest to you. This isn't a game, Harry. This killer is ruthless. I urge you to proceed with the greatest of caution."

"I appreciate the heads-up," I said.

Sometimes I forget Doc spends nearly all of his time chopping up corpses. I'm so used to seeing him doing it that I miss the fact that, when it comes to actual life-and-death situations, he's only there for the final credits, looking at the carnage but not participating in it. And I had to wonder how he would've advised Kate and me when we wandered into the hillbilly reunion not so long ago.

"Just thought it was worth underlining," he said. "After all, Doctor Polaski was trained the same way I am and I'm sure she certainly never gave that breakfast donut a second thought."

"Why would she?" I asked. "Why would anybody?"

"You're right, of course, Harry, but that doesn't mean you don't need to keep your wits about you. Ask yourself this: how did the killer get to the donuts without being seen at that time in the morning? Oh, and by the way, there are no security cameras. I checked."

I sighed, then said, "Thanks, Doc. I appreciate you letting us know." I was about to hang up when I thought of something. "Hey, while I've got you. We ran into Jacob Harper this morning. He gave us the go-ahead to do the exhumation should the need arise, and it's beginning to look as if we'll have no choice, but I'll let you know."

"Ah," Doc said. I couldn't tell if his tone was one of acceptance or curiosity. "Well, I'll certainly bear that in mind when I'm looking at my schedule in the upcoming weeks. Still no word on the examiner's report, I take it?"

"We've got one stop left," I said, rounding the front of the car and opening the driver's side door. "If that's a bust, you can grab your shovel."

"As I said, I'll bear it in mind. Talk to you later, Harry."

I heard a slight hesitation in his voice, as if for a moment he thought that I thought we were truly going to do this by hand. *Hah! Why not let him wonder,* I thought to myself, grinning a little. "Yes, later, Doc. I'll keep you up to date. Thanks again."

I ended the call and started the car. Jacque looked over at me. "We can't catch a break today, can we?"

I shrugged. "We're learning. We know it was cyanide that killed Polaski, which means we've kicked someone's dog and, taking the hoodie into account, we're being watched. It also means we have a live killer on the loose."

I pulled out onto the empty street. "Okay," I said, more forcefully than I intended, "I think we've beat around the bushes enough with the fathers. The chances they knew anything were slim, but we had to know. It's time we go back to the bureaucratic line. Let's go see what old Dick Wickam has to say."

"Bet you lunch that all we get is a load of nothing," Jacque said.

"How come?" I said and glanced over at her.

"We seem to be on a roll, is why. No one knows anything, and I don't see that changing," she said, pulling up the directions to the DA's office on the car's GPS.

I checked my watch as we walked through the glass doors at the entrance to Wickam's offices on the north side of the County Courthouse. It was almost three-thirty.

I shook my head. Whatever you might think about the government being there to serve the people, in my vast experience, they sure as hell made it a priority to get to the office after everyone else was at work, then high-tail it home before the whistle blew. That being said, we arrived just in time to catch him. Even so, I had my doubts he'd see us without an appointment. Appointments with DAs are, after all, about as useful as trying to corral a feral cat.

I held the door open for Jacque and she slipped inside, her voice already ringing out before my eyes had adjusted to the dim, professional lighting of the foyer.

"District Attorney Wickam," I heard her say. "What perfect timing." *How does she know it's him?* I wondered.

The expression on Wickam's face wasn't overly encouraging. He was standing by the receptionist's desk, a briefcase in one hand and a laptop bag slung over his shoulder. I smiled to myself. He'd been about thirty seconds too slow in dodging the meeting with the pesky detective from Chattanooga. *Tough luck, Dick.*

He glanced at Jacque, then at me, then at his watch. He had a split-second to come up with an excuse and thought he was going to make it. He opened his mouth to speak but then thought better of it, and the moment passed.

"We *so* appreciate you giving us a moment of time from your busy schedule," Jacque said, pouring on the accent and the charm. "And I promise we won't take up too much of your day. I can only imagine how many important t'ings you must have yet to accomplish."

Wow, now that's a little over the top, even for you, Jacque, I thought, inwardly smiling.

Watching Jacque work a mark was always fun. Her tone was a mix of Jamaican and almost air-headed charm, so perfectly down the middle that the DA would never be able to say for certain if he was being mocked or flattered. It sets people off balance, and she's used it effectively more times than I can count, especially on me.

"Yes," Wickam started, unsure of himself for what was probably one of very few times in his life. "I'm... just getting back in. I can give you a few minutes, of course. This way."

I glanced at the receptionist, and one look at her surprised expression was enough to confirm what I'd suspected. He was just getting somewhere, but it certainly wasn't into the office. Most likely, what he was getting in was his overpriced sports car to head to the country club and his cronies.

I don't hate lawyers as a rule, my father being one, after all, but sometimes perceptions aren't far off the mark. Wickam, in the ten seconds we'd seen him, was ticking all the boxes for a stereotypical stuffed shirt. I took a deep breath and followed him and Jacque down a hall to the office at the end.

Wickam's office was interchangeable with most of the high-level political ones I'd seen. The requisite large oak desk, paintings of presidents on the wall, and a sitting area in addition to chairs at the desk which was likely never used for anything. Or at least not anything he'd want his wife knowing about. He settled into a large, high-backed, maroon leather chair and crossed one leg over the other, his hands one on top of the other on his stomach, his sense of power reinstating itself as if it flowed from the very room we were now in.

He glanced surreptitiously at a blotter on the desk. "Mr. Starke, you said, and Miss... I'm sorry, I don't remember."

Jacque brushed off the obvious power play. "Jacque Hale."

"Ah, yes. Miss Hale. A pleasure to meet you both. So, what exactly is it I can do for you today?"

I knew he would expect me to take the reins, and as much as I would've liked to let Jacque give him the run-around, the day had begun to wear on me. If he was going to pretend to not know who we were or why we were there, *he* clearly had plenty of time to jerk us around. Most likely as some kind of childish revenge on us for catching him trying to dip out early.

"We just have a few questions about something that happened back in 2018," I said.

Given our meetings with Dill Harper and Eddy McDaniel, my guess was he knew everything we wanted to ask and had already practiced his answers. Coming at it from a roundabout angle was maybe the only way to throw him off balance. "Dill Harper asked me to say hello," I said, looking steadily at him across the desk.

He was a tall man, aged about fifty, his hair already graying at the sides. His well-trimmed mustache was also beginning to show a few gray hairs. A pair of steel-rimmed glasses would have completed the picture of a seriously serious counselor, except that he was wearing jeans and a white polo shirt.

Wickam frowned, lowered his head and stared at me over the rim of his glasses as if... Well, it was a pathetic attempt at pretending to think. "Who?"

"Oh, you know," Jacque spoke up. "Dill Harper. An older gentleman. He spoke glowingly of you. Said you're great friends. What was the phrase he used?" She looked over at me, still playacting. "Brothers in Christ?"

I nodded.

"Oh, *Dill* Harper," Wickam said, plastering on a smile. As if the name was an easy one to forget. "Yes. I know Dill. Wonderful man. Wonderful."

I waited for there to be more, but it seemed Wickam's approach was going to be one of empty words and pointless answers.

"He's actually the father of one of the two young men who died on the railroad tracks north of town," I said. "We've been hired to look into their deaths."

I paused, waiting to see if there would be a response. There was none.

"His son was Dillon Harper. I'm sure you remember the case."

"I do. What a shame... isn't it? I recall hearing about that..." Wickam trailed off, looking past us toward the window.

"A shame to be sure," I said. "And I can imagine you did hear about it. And you'll be hearing more about it. We're here to talk with the parents of the two young men, and we had an appointment to meet with Brenda Polaski."

"Polaski..." he said, frowning. "You mean—"

"The medical examiner," Jacque said, her pretenses gone. "She worked the deaths of the two young men, Dillon Harper and Brian McDaniel."

Wickam looked at her for a moment, apparently genuinely surprised to see the young woman in front of him run out of patience so quickly. "Well, if she worked the case, then she shouldn't be hard to find. The ME's office isn't far from here; it's on Chambliss. I can give you the address if you like."

"We were there this morning, Mr. Wickam. Apparently, you haven't heard. Doctor Polaski is dead. She was murdered sometime between seven-thirty and eight."

"*What?* No... *No!*" Wickam's face paled.

"Yes, actually," I said. "I can't believe Chief Snow hasn't already informed you."

He was shaking his head, obviously stunned by the news.

"That's... that's... awful," he said.

"The problem is, counselor, other than her death, Doctor Polaski had promised to help us with our investigation. But now that she's no longer with us, we thought you might be able to help us. You signed off on Doctor Polaski's report, did you not?"

"If you say I did," he replied with a sigh.

Clearly, he was in another world and had lost interest in us.

"Well, we do say," Jacque said. "And since it's getting late, and you obviously need to be elsewhere, how about we make this as quick and easy as possible?"

Her tone was sharp and that bothered me.

Wickam looked almost as if he'd been waiting for it. Even the slightest amount of spirit from someone he no doubt considered his inferior was enough for him to enlist the power of his office and shut things down.

"Well, then, if I signed it, *miss*," he emphasized the word, "then clearly I agreed with her findings and have nothing more to add. I don't know what happened to Doctor Polaski. And I barely recall the case in question. I'm sure you must have seen her report, so what, exactly, is it you want from me?"

"That's the problem," I said. "We haven't seen the report. No one seems to know where it is. Chief Snow's file is incomplete. We were hoping you have a copy we could see."

He stared at me for a moment, then said, "Yes, I'm sure we do. But I don't have time to go look for it today. I'll have Jenny look for it tomorrow and get back to you." And with that, Wickam stood up, sending us a clear message that the interview was over.

I stood up, held out my hand, and said, "That would be perfect. Thank you, and thank you for your time, Mr. Wickam. We'll be on our way."

Wickam nodded, shook my hand and said, "You're welcome. Come, I'll show you out." He looked at Jacque, who was also on her feet, and said, "It was nice to meet you, too, Miss Hale."

I shot her a look. I could see her eyes flashing, and she was smiling. I'd known her long enough to know a fake smile when I saw one.

"You as well," she said, the accent thick off her tongue. "You have a nice rest of d'day."

And two minutes later, we were back out on the street.

"People like that," she said, looking up at the sky. "I swear, Harry. If you ever..."

Whatever she said next faded into the background as I looked across the street. A dark blue SUV was idling at the curb. Any other time it wouldn't have been so conspicuous, but after what had happened to Brenda Polaski that morning, I was on high alert.

I looked at Jacque. She was still muttering under her breath about all the things she would've liked to have said. "Hop in," I said, breaking her stream of thought.

She gave me an odd look but got in the car, then said, "I'm not wrong, Harry. You do know that, right?"

I waved it away.

"Across the street," I said. "To my right. A dark blue SUV. Can you see it?"

She leaned back to look past my shoulder. "Is that..."

"Our hoodie friend?" I said. "Yes, I think it is."

18

Wednesday, 3:15pm

"SHOULD WE GO TALK TO HIM?" JACQUE ASKED AS SHE stared across the road at the SUV.

I thought for a moment. "Maybe. He hasn't really done anything other than be where we are, though. At least not yet. For all we know, he may not know he's been made."

"Scenic route, then?" she asked.

I smiled. "You think? It's not like I know my way around Cleveland." I shook my head, then said, "Okay, let's give it a try."

I pulled out onto the street—that would be 2nd Street going west—crossed over Broad, took a right on Worth, a left on 6th, left again on Oak Street, then left again on Inman and pulled into the front lot of a muffler shop and parked, the engine running.

Two minutes later, we watched as the SUV cruised by, the

driver doing everything he could to look as nonchalant as possible. And thereby making himself even more noticeable.

Jacque laughed. "He may as well have been twiddling his thumbs and whistling Dixie. 'Nothin' to see here, boss. Just drivin' around in circles as usual.'"

I pulled back out onto Inman and took after him, looked at Jacque and said, "You didn't get the plate number, I suppose?"

"No," she said. "The glare of the sun off the back window was in my eyes."

"Yeah, me too," I said.

I was three cars behind him. "Damn it," I snarled as he cruised through a red light and the cars in front of us stopped. Needless to say, when the lights turned green, he was long gone.

"Shi...eesh," I said and banged the wheel in frustration. "Damn it!" I sighed. "Well, that's that. Though, I don't think we've seen the last of him."

Jacque laughed. "It's been one of those days, Harry."

"I was just thinking about Brenda Polaski's donuts," I said as I eased through the light and turned right onto Ocoee, heading south. "I wonder where she bought them... if she bought them?"

"There's no telling where those came from. Grocery store, donut shop, bakery, even a gas station. Wait..." She turned to me in her seat. "Did you see the box?"

"I didn't," I said, realizing we may have missed something staring right in our faces. But almost as quickly, I dismissed it. "But Doc Sheddon did. That man lives for a good mystery. If there had been anything worth noting, he would've seen it and called us." I tossed her my phone. "Shoot him a text."

While Jacque typed, I headed out to APD-40, took a right and headed toward the Interstate. And, as I drove in silence, I thought back through the day. It had been a busy one and, despite all our efforts, not a very productive one. Brenda was starting to look more and more like the only person who could've been able to give us something tangible to go on. Unfortunately, though, someone else had thought so, too, and got to her before we did.

"You know," I began, but she held up a finger, looking at the phone.

"Doc says it was a Krispy Kreme box purchased at Publix. Cellophane window in lid. Housed one half dozen donuts, two raspberry, two chocolate-iced, and two glazed, one of which had been half-eaten. He's sending it to check for fingerprints. No distinguishing markings other than the Publix label. Maybe we'll get lucky and they'll find a print with a match." She handed the phone back to me.

"I wouldn't hold your breath. If someone's going to go to that much trouble, they're not going to leave prints on the box. Here." I handed the phone back to her. "See if you can find the Publix."

She quickly found it. "It's just off Paul Huff Parkway."

"There you go," I said. "The chances of identifying someone out of several thousand supermarket customers at that time in the morning is zero to none, especially if we don't know who we're looking for."

"Hoodie, d'you think?"

I thought for a moment. "I doubt it. It would have to be someone she knew. He doesn't seem the type, though we never did get a good look at his face."

"They've got to screw up sooner or later," she said.

"They always do, don't they?" I replied.

We drove on several miles in silence before I spoke again. I'm an expert at letting the wheels in my head spin, and I'd been doing too much of that at home. Amanda needed a break from it as much as anyone else did, and since I had Jacque, I decided to kick around some thoughts.

"The guy in the SUV," I said. "We didn't pick him up till Eddy McDaniel's place, right?"

She tapped her finger on her chin as she thought. "Not that I know of. But I wasn't looking for anyone either. If he hadn't been standing out there for God and everybody else to see, I don't know if we'd have noticed him at all."

"Right," I said. "But for the sake of argument, let's say he wasn't there. After all, at that point, we'd made two stops, right? One to see Brenda, then one to see Dill."

"But when we got to Eddy's, he already knew we were in town," she said, finishing my thought.

"Exactly. So somewhere along the line, we picked up our tail, and I'd almost bet it was sooner than we like to think."

"How come?"

"Because the most important meeting of the day, in hindsight, was the one that we didn't have. When we left this morning, who was your money on for the most help?"

"Out of the four?" she said, then paused for a moment. "Brenda, I guess. It was odd that she wouldn't tell you anything over the phone, so she might have just been giving you the runaround. The cloak-and-dagger stuff about the appointment definitely raised some red flags, though. From what you've told me, I'd say she was going to fess up to some kind of malpractice. Or whatever you call it when the person is already dead."

"Right," I said. "We didn't know if she was going to be a waste of our time or not, but apparently someone else did. So, they eliminated her before she had the chance to spill her guts."

"And then they just sit back to see what we do," she said.

"We go to Dill Harper first," I said.

"And that pretty well indicated we're going to track down the parents," she said.

"So they know Eddy McDaniel will be next. If they knew we would go to the DA or not is irrelevant, as all they had to do was sit back and watch. But I'm betting they had our day just about as well planned out as we did."

"It was easy enough to figure it out when you look back on it, isn't it?" she said, sounding almost disappointed.

"We had no reason to think our meeting with Brenda was anything other than a... meeting," I said. "Don't beat yourself up over it. The question is, though, who was keeping tabs on us?"

"It's gotta be a pretty short list," she said. "The police chief and... I don't know, Harry, but it has to be a really short list."

"That's the problem," I said. "There has to be more people involved in this than we know. And, like the guy or not, do you really see Wickam getting himself wrapped up in a double-murder?"

"Yeah, I do. Nasty..." She paused. "It wouldn't surprise me at all, and it would be three bodies if we're counting Brenda... But maybe we shouldn't be counting her at all."

"What do you mean?" I asked.

She thought for a moment and then turned in her seat to look at me. "Okay, so just bear with me because I know this is a long shot. But what if the person who killed Brenda Polaski *is* Brenda Polaski?"

"Like a suicide?"

"Maybe," she said. "Maybe she picked a quick death. And she set up an appointment only to kill herself moments before we got there, ensuring we'd find the body. She's a doctor, so she'd have access to cyanide."

"Okay, for the sake of argument, I'll bite. What about the intern, though? How could she make sure the other lady didn't die?"

"Maybe it was only one donut she poisoned. She could've bought the box herself, added a little spice, took a bite and went about her business."

I watched the dashed lines tick by on the highway. "It's possible," I said finally, "but I'm not sure I can get fully onboard. Granted, I need to reread *Deadly Poisons and How to Put Them on Donuts*, but wouldn't there be a risk of cross-contamination? Besides, if you're going to kill yourself, why so many other factors? Why make the meeting if you know the intern will be there? Or vice-versa, why have the intern come in and risk her exposure if she only wanted us to find her? And then there's the type of death. I mean, Doc said it was quick, but a minute can seem like a very long time."

"Okay, but..." Jacque sat for a moment and then threw up her hands. "All right. It's a long shot. I just go round and round with things like this, and I wanted to at least get some of the crazy thoughts out of my head."

I smiled. "I know exactly what you mean. Don't worry about it. We have to come at this from every possible angle and, right now, it's looking more and more like a case we're only going to solve by removing possibilities. We just don't have enough to go on."

"I suppose you're going to nix Dill Harper as well," she said.

I chuckled. "He may not have liked his son, but somehow I don't see Dill killing him."

"Maybe he thought he was saving him," she said. "Send him to Heaven before he can do something that would have gotten him sent to Hell."

"It's happened," I said, thinking back on an old case study I'd read years ago. Some guy murdered his entire family to get them a straight shot to the pearly gates. It was all the rage in philosophical and ethical debates at the time. Was his motive justified, was his religion to blame, yadda yadda. It always seemed to me, unless someone is on fire, putting a bullet in them isn't going to do them much good. But, who knows? "The problem here is, of course, that we still have Brenda Polaski to deal with. Who would have a motive to kill her, and what was that motive?"

"To shut her up, of course," Jacque said.

"I dunno. No! You're right. She knew something, and she was going to spill it to us. She must have known those two kids were murdered. But did she know who done it? That's the question, my dear Watson. Eh, maybe I'm missing something."

Jacque sighed. "I don't know if marking off the possibilities is going to help us any either. I can come up with a whole lot of them if you give me time enough."

"True," I said. "But you can toss them out just as quickly. We're not done with this one yet. Besides, we've still got TJ and Heather to talk to. They may have found an angle."

"I hope so," she said. "Because after today, all I can think about is how much I do and do not want a donut."

I laughed. "That's it?"

"Well... Yes, I suppose."

I dropped Jacque back by her car in the office parking lot and, seeing no other vehicles in the lot, turned home with a grateful sigh. It had been some kind of a day, and I was ready for it to end.

I knew I wasn't going to get this thing straightened out; there were only so many hours I could spend kicking around the same thoughts over and over again.

I drove home that afternoon, trying to put things behind me for the evening and focus on the family that was waiting for me.

Amanda and Jade were already getting settled down for dinner, a routine we'd quickly learned was crucial if we were going to have our daughter get any amount of food into her mouth before the meal was done. Jade kept both of us entertained and wore herself down at the same time, yawning through most of her bath and then dropping off to sleep the moment her head hit the pillow.

Amanda met me down on the couch in the living room again for what was starting to feel like our own bedtime routine.

"No luck?" she asked, sitting down and leaning her back against my shoulder.

"Yes and no," I said. "Mostly no."

Amanda was quiet, letting me continue, I assumed.

"But, you know how these things work," I said. "The only way to get away with a crime is to disappear. This one is just slowly branching out. Sooner or later something will turn up."

"Branching out how?" She twisted around to look at me.

I gave her a quick rundown of what had happened at the ME's office and Dr. Polaski's untimely demise, doing my best to downplay as much as I could, though there is little you can do to make death by cyanide sound pedestrian.

"I know you hate to hear this," she said when I was done, "and I know how good you are at ignoring what you don't like, but you need to be careful on this one."

"Because of the junk food?" I tried to joke.

"Actually, yes," she said. "Getting shot or stabbed or run over, those are all terrible, and I'm not trying to blow them off. But this is a... connivingly wicked way to kill someone. It's sneaky and it's clever, and it's something a woman would do."

And I thought about Asabelle Kitner, the intern. *Surely not!*

I put the thought out of my head, rubbed her hair and kissed the top of her head. She wasn't too far wrong. I've never been a fan of having a gun pointed at me, but at least that kind of danger is clear and explicit. Killings like this one were almost impossible to see until it was too late.

"But also," she said, filling the silence, "about the junk food. Specifically, if you're having some, I expect you to share."

I laughed, slipping out from under her arm and tucking a throw cushion under her head. "You know, I think there might be some ice cream in the freezer. It sounds like just the thing we need."

She laughed. "Now there's a plan I can get on board with."

19

Thursday morning, 8am

I ARRIVED EARLY AT THE OFFICE THE NEXT MORNING. I WAS hoping to spend some time sorting through any reports or files that Tim might've dug up, as well as check on a few other angles that might give us something to work with. I'd spent most of the night keeping the case at bay, but once Amanda and I had gone to bed, it was only a few hours before I found my eyes open in the dark and ideas bouncing around inside my skull.

I'd slept at least, albeit fitfully, but not until I'd finally figured out what it was that was bothering me so much. It wasn't Brenda Polaski's death, nor was it DA Wickam's off-putting personality. It was something we'd left entirely on the back burner in our flurry of interviews the day before. Yes, I'd missed it; Tim had not.

I started a pot of coffee and sat down at my desk to see a case file neatly placed at the center where I'd be sure to see it. I opened the folder and looked down at what Tim had barely mentioned previously—but had apparently come back to again and again while the rest of us had been out doing our interviews.

Greg Sneed.

I read through what little information there was and started to wonder if there really was anything so out of the ordinary about our missing ME report. We were now two-for-two on bare-bones case files. Granted, Greg Sneed's situation was a little less cut and dried than the deaths we were already looking into, but it still left me wanting more.

On the surface, Sneed's case didn't really have anything to set it apart from thousands of others just like it that get filed across the country every year. Greg had gone missing and, at least as far as the file was concerned, that was the last anyone had to say about it. In all fairness, though, sometimes there just wasn't anything else to say. People have all kinds of reasons for not wanting to be found, and not all of them imply anything criminal. Shoot, it would be difficult to find anyone who hadn't, at one time or another, thought about how much easier things would be if they could just uproot themselves and transplant to a new place and start over. L&L, I've heard it called; liquidate and leave. Granted, those who actually do so are few and far between, but something being rare doesn't make it a crime when it does happen. Was that what happened to Greg?

For some vague reason, I didn't think so. Greg's case felt different somehow. I looked through the details again, making notes as I went. Perhaps the one thing that made his case stand out was its proximity to the deaths we were already investigating. Greg's missing person report was filed only a month after our boys died on the tracks. Again, that wasn't anything major by itself. Coincidences happen more often than we like to admit. But also, again, it was proximity.

The deaths of Brian and Dillon were, for lack of a better word, unusual. And a missing person, while it's common on the larger scale of things, is usually a local buzz, especially in a town the size of Cleveland. For both of these situations to arise, both in time and place and so close to each other, was something that didn't fit the standard pattern for out-of-the-ordinary situations.

I looked back up to the top of the file to see who'd been the investigating officer and wasn't entirely surprised to see a familiar name: Detective Louise Baker, current resident of the great state of Alaska. I wanted it to mean more than it did, but if I was going to be fair about coincidences, then again, the size of Cleveland had to be taken into consideration. She probably had her name on dozens, if not hundreds, of pages in the Cleveland police files. But still, it didn't sit entirely well with me. Something made her transfer out, and I just couldn't believe it was the weather.

Or maybe, if I was being honest with myself, the weather was the one thing making me hope to find a way I could write her out of this whole thing. I'd dealt with plenty of people like her in the past and, while they might be full of bluster and curtness on the phone, in person, staring eye-to-eye with their interrogator, they tend to take on a different attitude. And that's all well and good when I can just run down to a local address and find who I need. But, Alaska... I almost shivered just thinking about it.

Before I could convince myself one way or the other, though, I heard voices out in the lobby and Heather knocked on my door, opened it and poked her head inside.

"Now a good time?" she asked, a bright smile on her face.

"Come on in," I said. "TJ with you?"

The man slipped in behind Heather as she walked over to one of the chairs in front of my desk. If Heather was always upbeat, TJ was always a brick wall. He merely nodded and sat down across from me.

"So what's the word?" I asked, looking back and forth between them. "You sounded as if you had a pretty interesting encounter yesterday."

Heather nodded. "Definitely interesting, though if you had the impression we were gonna hand you the solution to this thing on a silver platter, don't get your hopes up just yet."

"I'm not in the habit of doing that, as you should know," I said, thinking of my conversation with Jacque the afternoon previous. "Start from the top."

"Well, as you know," Heather began, "Alan Woodward is currently in the county lockup on an A&B. Nothing really out of the ordinary. Just another bar fight at a honky-tonk in rural Tennessee. You think they'd come up with a way around those by now. Assault and Battery just sounds a little over the top for a series of windmill punches, don't you think?

"But that's neither here nor there," she continued. "The point is, he's been cooling off for a while now and seems to be pretty well used to his current abode. He's not a career criminal by any stretch of the imagination, but you find me a good old boy who hasn't at least seen the drunk tank once and I'll show you a liar. In our opinion," she said and glanced at TJ for confirmation, "he's just a pretty run-of-the-mill young man with a hot temper. If he hadn't been associated with our two victims, I don't think you'd ever hear his name."

"All right," I said. "That makes sense. Neither Brian nor Dillon had much of a name for themselves, either; good or bad."

"Exactly," she said. "To hear him tell it, Alan was mostly upset about the fact that he wasn't there with his buddies. Survivor's guilt kind of thing. If he had been there, maybe he could've done something... so on and so forth."

"What exactly were they up to?" I asked. "No one's been able to give me a good answer on even a basic detail yet. Unless we're going with drunkenly wandering onto the train tracks, that is."

Heather folded her hands in her lap and shrugged. Like Jacque, she had a wide variety of personas she could take on when the situation required it. Typically my office wasn't one that required any bit of playacting, so her almost school-girl-ish pose and response seemed to be unconscious more than anything else.

"Kinda yes, kinda no," she said. "The way Woodward explained it, the three of them were initially going to meet up and go out for a sunset hunt. Not exactly legal, but at this point, I think we can all pretty much let that one slide. I mean, talking about it isn't a crime. Even if we did want to go after him about it for some strange reason, I'd really advise against it."

"Why's that?" I asked.

"He talks," TJ said, finally breaking his silence, though he just as quickly settled back into it.

"Exactly," Heather said. "You never know what you're going to get when you walk into a county lockup, but to be honest, Woodward's a pleasant guy, and we got the impression he genuinely wanted to help and wasn't concerned about how it might look to the other inmates in the process." Again, she looked at TJ for confirmation. He merely nodded.

"He said he was ready to talk whenever we wanted to if it would help find out what happened to his buddies."

"He doesn't exactly have a busy schedule," I pointed out.

"I know," Heather responded. "But you know how those interviews can go. Those boys from out in the county like to pretend they're in the big leagues, and giving us a hard time is the easiest way to impress their buddies. Not him, though."

I nodded. "Fair point. So they were going to go out hunting…" I trailed off, suddenly remembering something Jacob had said when Jacque and I had crossed paths with him at the diner. "Did he say anything about how they were going to hunt? Shotgun, maybe?"

Heather pointed at me, a smile on her face. "Exactly. Nice work, boss. He said they'd all met up earlier in the evening, but Dillon was late on account of having to find his brother's shotgun. Apparently, none of the three actually owned a gun—"

"Or a license to use one, most likely," TJ said.

"And Jacob Harper had given Dillon permission to use his whenever he wanted," Heather continued. "According to Woodward, Jacob had joined the marines a while previous and Dillon would latch onto whatever his brother had left lying around."

I nodded. "Everything seems to match up with what I've heard so far."

"Well," Heather said, "this is where it might veer off a little. It seems that, while Alan Woodward was all gung ho to go out with his friends that night, something came up that convinced him to do otherwise. Care to guess what it was?"

I laughed. "I can think of only one thing that would come between a guy and his buddies."

"Exactly," she said. "He'd found himself a new lady friend, and apparently, she'd decided she was in need of his... attention that evening. So, seeing as how he was already with Brian and Dillon, the three of them had a few beers, and then Woodward took off for his romantic rendezvous."

"Any reason why we shouldn't believe this?" I asked, looking in particular at TJ. If anyone was going to sniff out a lie, it would've been him.

His response was quick. "Seemed reasonable to me."

I tapped my pen on the desk. "All right. So Woodward splits. He can't know what happened later, so what else can he have to tell us that's worth anything? It sounds to me as if he's as much in the dark as we are."

"I agree," Heather said, "but that's the thing. Just because he wasn't there doesn't mean he can't shine some light on the mystery. After all, he knew these guys better than we ever will."

"So what was his take on what happened? So far, according to the fathers at least, Dillon was a loose cannon and Brian was struggling with some pretty intense demons."

"The mother and sister?" Heather asked. "Yeah, talk about a tragedy. But it's interesting because, according to Woodward, Brian was handling it well. Or as well as one could expect. Brian was working through it," she continued. "He even had a job lined up down in Alabama and was supposed to be leaving." She sighed. "That's what made this so weird, Harry. The person who was supposed to be depressed, Brian, was actually looking like he was on the upswing. Dillon? Well, I can't say one way or the other, but Woodward didn't seem nearly as concerned about him as his dad was. But I also feel like that's a pretty standard situation with ultra-religious families. To be honest, the only one who really seemed to be dealing with mental health issues is Woodward himself."

"Meaning?" I asked, waiting for the other shoe to drop, for her to tell me that Woodward had a few screws loose and couldn't be trusted.

"Meaning, it seems like he's carrying around a lot of survivor's guilt." I opened my mouth to speak, but she held up her hand.

"Wait," she said. "I know what you're thinking, and it crossed my mind too. But he's lucid. The conversation was clear-headed. I think Alan still feels bad that there might have been something he could've done if he'd been there, but he's dealing with it."

I rested my chin on my hand, tapping the pen on the paper with the other. "So how did this level-headed guy end up in jail?"

"I said he's dealing with it," Heather repeated. "As in, he hadn't before. That's one of the other reasons I'm inclined to put a lot of stock in his assessment. He's definitely gotten himself under control and seems to have a pretty realistic grasp on his own behavior. The guilt might pass, it might not, but he's not acting out and he's not irrational."

"It happens," TJ added, and I knew there were numerous stories behind those two short words.

"It seems like he would've let this go by now, though," I said. "Don't you think? If he's making such leaps in his own mental health, there might be something else holding him back. As far as he knows, or should know, it was just a case of them being in the wrong place at the wrong time."

"I asked that," she said. "He said it's not just that something happened. It was... how'd he put it?" She glanced at TJ.

"Said if it'd been a drunk driving accident, that'd be one thing. But he'd told 'em more'n once not to be too comfortable out by the railway yard, especially Cooperman's."

"Because?"

TJ shrugged, and I looked at Heather.

"This is the part that's a little tricky," she said. "He didn't really know why to stay away or what you'd be avoiding by doing so, but apparently a friend of his knew about something shady going on out there and had given him, Woodward, the heads-up. Then, when he realized how much Brian and Dillon liked to wander the property, he'd told them, too. Of course, all it did was make them want to go there even more. At least, that's what he said."

And there it was. It had taken a while, but she'd finally gotten to it, and it was important.

"Hmm... So the plot thickens," I said. "What was going on at the old industrial park, I wonder? Who's the friend, and were you able to track him down?"

"Well," Heather said, "yes and no. We looked for him, but talking to him... well, that's going to be a little more difficult."

"Why's that?"

"No one knows where he is," she said. "He's missing."

I frowned. "Another one? What's his name?"

"Greg Sneed," she said.

Bam! I'd slammed my pen down on the desk. "You've got to be kidding me."

Heather looked shocked at my response. TJ, not so much.

"Sorry," I said. "That wasn't something I was expecting to hear." I looked at my watch. It was getting on for nine.

"See if you can find his parents," I said, "the mother in particular. She's the one who filed his MPR. That boy's either dead or he's on the run, and I want to know which. If he's on the run, we need to find him."

"On it," Heather said as the two of them stood up.

"And guys," I said, "get everything you can, even if it doesn't seem relevant. You never know. We've got a lot of work ahead of us here, and I don't want to waste any more time than we already have. The useless information we can sort out, but we can't put the evidence together until we have it all."

TJ nodded, and they exited the room. Me, I stared down at my notebook, tapping the tip of my pen on my desk.

The name I'd scribbled down earlier seemed to stare back at me, mocking me.

"Greg Sneed," I muttered. "Greg... Sneed!"

20

Thursday morning, 10:15am

I STARED AT THE NAME FOR A LONG TIME, MY MIND IN A whirl, random thoughts flitting through the maelstrom like birds tossed on the wind, none of them making any sense. But once again, my so-called sixth sense was telling me that Greg was long dead and buried.

Finally, I sighed and gave up. I glanced again at the time and was surprised to see it was just after ten. Which meant it was just after six in Anchorage. And I figured that might work in my favor. I needed to try and talk to Detective Baker again, but now, with the possibility that the guys were armed the night of their deaths, I wanted more than just a rehashing of what was slowly turning up. I needed to know why it was taking so much effort to track down facts that should've been relevant and noted in the file. Too much was missing or unaccounted for—from the ME's report to Greg Sneed.

The odds were that Baker was just getting up, but with any luck, she wouldn't be quite out of bed yet. Either way, I was almost positive she would answer. Police officers spend too much time in risky situations to leave much to chance. If a phone rings, you answer it, not because you expect it to be something bad, but because you've been conditioned to realize how quickly and how often things can go south. Plus, whether you're clocked in or not, anyone who knows you're an officer will likely make you their first call, even if, and sometimes especially, they ought to be calling the station first. It's the comfort of the familiar.

When you're the one looking down at the phone screen, though, nine times out of ten, it's just another unsaved number you're seeing. For a cop, that doesn't mean much. Outside of saving the entire phone book in your contacts list, you're going to get unknown numbers more often than not. My hope was that I was still an Unknown on her cell and not saved. She might not ignore an unfamiliar number, but after our last chat, the name "Harry Starke" on her screen would guarantee a trip to voicemail.

I tapped in her number, hit send, and counted the number of rings.

Halfway through the fourth ring, she picked up, sounding like she hadn't even kicked off the covers yet. I can't say I would've blamed her. The pre-dawn hours in Anchorage must be a little nippy.

"Baker," she said before clearing her throat and trying again. "This is Louise Baker."

"Detective Baker," I said, avoiding any kind of joviality or small talk. I needed her brain to kick straight into work mode before she had time to think about it. "This is Harry Starke. We got off to a bad start last time, but I really do need to talk to you about the deaths of Dillon Harper and Brian McDaniel in Cleveland. You handled the case, so I assume you remember it. I need you to clarify just one detail for me and I'll let you go. Was there a firearm recovered at the scene? Specifically, a shotgun? It would've belonged to the brother of one of the victims."

"Who? I..."

It was good. I could almost see her scrambling to recall the facts of the case instead of considering if she should even be discussing them.

"A firearm... no... I'm sorry... It was years ago."

I imagined her shaking her head, wiping the sleep from her eyes. The first answer was good, honest, and pertinent. But I knew my window was closing rapidly.

"I have a witness who stated that they intended to go hunting that evening and that they had a twelve-gauge shotgun with them. And you're confirming that no such weapon was found?"

"Yes. I mean, no. Yes, I'm confirming there was no weapon." She cleared her throat, and I knew it was probably the end of any easy answers I would get out of her. "I'm sorry. Who is this again? Starke?"

"Harry Starke, ma'am," I said. "We spoke previously about the case and the lack of information. That hasn't changed. There's still a glaring lack of information. Considering that you were the investigating officer, I'm hoping you can help me out."

"I said we didn't find a weapon," she almost growled. However, I'd caught her; she was wide awake now, and this certainly wasn't how she had hoped to start her day. Given our last inter-action, I wasn't entirely upset to know I'd gotten under her skin.

"Fine," I said. "So let's put that aside for now. I have a couple more questions, and I'd like answers."

She was silent for a moment, then said quietly, "I suggest you rethink whatever it is you're doing, Mr. Starke. You're swimming in deep waters. Be careful you don't get swept away."

"So you say," I replied, hoping that if I couldn't keep her sleepy, I might irritate her into saying something more. "But I've been hired to do a job, and I intend to do it. When I called before, I was looking for the ME's report. I'm still looking for it."

"Really?" she said sarcastically. "Now why am I not surprised?"

"That's an interesting response," I said. "Care to clarify?"

"Care to clarify..." She sighed, annoyed. "What are you again? A PI? I hope you don't charge too much for your services. If a sheet of paper went missing five years ago, why should I be surprised it's still missing? No one's been looking for it other than you, I'd almost bet. And, whatever you think of your own capabilities, a few days isn't likely to undo a few years' worth of mess. Ask the ME. If you'll recall, Cleveland isn't in my jurisdiction anymore."

"Funny you should say that," I said. "I was going to do just that. I even had a meeting set up with Brenda Polaski, and at her own request, no less. Care to guess what happened there?"

"You kept hounding her, and she got fed up and decided not to talk to you?"

"Wrong," I said. "Brenda Polaski was murdered about five minutes before I arrived. Someone slipped a little cyanide into her breakfast. Not the most subtle way to go about it, don't you think?"

The pause told me I'd finally gotten her full attention.

"So what I'm thinking," I continued quickly, "is that you're now the only person still alive who really knows what happened that night, and I assure you I take very little joy in hounding you like this. But if you want it to stop, all you have to do is answer my questions and I'll get out of your hair."

She laughed, but it wasn't out of amusement. It was almost a pitying sound. "You PIs. Fancy yourselves as modern-day gunslingers, don't you? Just push hard enough and we poor souls have to give in and fall in line. Well, I'll tell you this one more time, Mr. Starke, and after this, I hope you'll stop bugging me and not expect me to answer any more of your calls. Are you listening? Good. Believe me when I tell you you're already in over your head. You have no idea what you're messing with. Let it go. Let the past stay in the past. If you keep pushing, it's not going to end well for you."

"Is that a threat, detective?"

"From me? Of course not. You think I came up here for my health? I'm just giving you the facts. You keep poking this bear, eventually it's going to wake up, and what happens after that..." She trailed off. "Alaska is a pretty square deal as far as I'm concerned. As for Brenda? Sounds to me like the bear's already awake."

"Give me something, Louise," I said, trying a different angle. "Whatever happened to you, it can't have been good. Point me in the right direction and I'll see what I can do to make things right for you." It wasn't entirely true, but I needed to at least pretend to give her the benefit of the doubt.

"All you can do for me is to leave me alone," she said, almost resignedly. "What happens to you is on your own head now."

"Just a name," I said. "Anything."

There was a long pause. I glanced at the screen. Just like that, without a final word, she'd hung up on me, again.

I looked at the phone for a moment; the sudden urge to throw it across the office at the wall was almost overwhelming. It's one thing to hit dead ends during an investigation. It's so par for the course that if it doesn't happen early on, you start to wonder if you've made a mistake. Or are being set up. But this, to have the phone number of the person who had the information, to have them pointedly refuse to give it to you, well, there's nothing more frustrating.

I glanced at the clock again as if the call had taken much longer than the few minutes I knew it had. TJ and Heather would likely barely be out of the parking lot, but I was already antsy for them to get back and report on Greg Sneed's mother. If this woman in Alaska wasn't going to help, I had to find another way to get the information I needed.

I tossed the phone on the desk, frustrated, realizing that, had I been any other investigator in town, this stonewalling might have worked. What Louise Baker wasn't considering, though, was that I had both the persistence and the means to force the issue. If she wasn't going to answer my calls, then maybe I'd take a little flight up to Alaska and meet with her face-to-face. It wasn't the ideal solution, but maybe the shock of my turning up on her doorstep would shake something out of her.

I leaned back in my chair and took a couple of deep breaths, taking a moment to think about it. I'd done a lot of things following my gut, and a lot of them had turned out well. Maybe flying to Alaska out of spite would be one of them. But, I reminded myself, it was a lot of hours from Chattanooga to

Anchorage, no matter how you went about it. So, for the time being, I figured my best bet was to sit tight and find out what I could from Mrs. Sneed. After that, we could consider the exhumation. But one way or another, I wasn't going to let Detective Baker off the hook quite so easily.

21

Thursday morning, 11:45am

I spent the better part of the next two hours tying up some loose ends and filling out the paperwork that always lingers long after a case has been closed. It's the nuts and bolts of being a PI. And, as much as I wanted to devote all my time to the railroad case, I also knew I couldn't just beat the pages to death and expect something to come leaping out of them. Besides, these infidelities and runaways were what made it possible to tackle the trickier situations.

For every fifteen cases I took on, fourteen of them would be solved within a few days and that would be the end of it. Life just isn't as mysterious as folks like to believe. But those easy successes, while they made the difficult cases like this one more interesting, also tended to make the puzzles linger longer in my mind.

I know I'm no Sherlock Holmes, but I do have a knack for reading people, learning from experience, and piecing things together. When something gets stuck in my mind, it irritates me in all kinds of ways. And this case took me way beyond that.

So, it was with more than a little relief that I saw Heather's car pull back into the lot a little before noon. I quickly closed up the case files I was working on and made ready to tackle the real mystery.

The pair entered in their usual fashion: Heather all smiles, TJ looking like he hadn't felt an emotion in two decades, which, if I'm being honest, he probably hadn't.

They sat down. Looked at one another. I uncapped my fountain pen and looked at them across the desk.

"All right," I said. "Give me some good news."

"Good news might be a little bit of a stretch," Heather started, "but it's definitely not bad news. At least not that I can see. Think of it as more like mildly pleasing news and we'll be on the same page."

I nodded. "Mildly pleasing will do, for now." I couldn't help it. I rolled my eyes.

"Well," she said, "on the plus side, when we got to the residence, it wasn't just the mother who was there. We got to meet both parents, meaning we won't have to spend time tracking down any other Sneeds." She paused, looked at TJ, then at me.

"Anyway," she continued, waving a hand, "the mother and father were both more than happy to talk to us, though it may take a little bit of sorting to figure out which bits are true, and which are more true because the parents want to believe they are."

"Nothing out of the ordinary there," I said. "Parents tend to look on the bright side. What is it they're trying to gloss over?"

"It's not entirely clear," Heather said thoughtfully. "I don't think they were trying to pull the wool over their own eyes, and, to their credit, they didn't try to beat around the bush either. Did you think?" She looked at TJ, who merely shook his head no. "Both mom and dad were pretty confident Greg had gotten himself involved in the drug scene one way or another. Then again, if we're being honest... that shouldn't surprise us."

"True," I said. East Tennessee is no different from anywhere else in these United States. Drug use is prevalent, and someone has to supply the demand, and that usually means organized crime, whether it be a large organization or a small one. Even when the usage was as recreational as folks like to pretend, or something worse. Fentanyl's as much a problem in Chattanooga as it is in Chicago, and I have no doubt, in Cleveland, TN, too.

"How involved?" I asked.

"Neither of his parents thought he was actually using, nor did either of them balk at the idea that he could've been dealing."

"Dealing or distributing?"

Heather took a breath, thinking. "My gut says dealing. I think if he would've been big-time, they would've caught on. It's hard to keep that kind of operation hidden."

I knew enough to trust her about that. And she was right. Even if you try to keep living the same, low-key life, the influx of product and the large amounts of money to be made in the drug distribution makes it hard to say no to yourself, especially when there's no real reason to. It's why you see so many top-of-the-line cars outside of ramshackle homes. Buying a new house seems flashy, but getting a nice car somehow feels less so. Or at least that's what I've been told.

"Either way," Heather continued, "the Sneeds weren't too concerned about keeping secrets, so whatever they knew, I think they genuinely told us. In fact, they said they'd be willing to hire us to look into Greg's disappearance as well."

I raised an eyebrow.

"I told her we would discuss it and get back to her," she said.

"Fair enough," I said. "I have a feeling we may very well find out what happened to Greg without having to work too hard."

"That's kind of what I thought," Heather said. "But, whether we take the case or not, she did give us this." Heather reached into her jacket pocket and pulled out a little notebook. "It's Greg's little black book. There's a whole list of names for us to look into. What do you bet there's some overlap here?"

"Interesting," I said. "Anyone there we know?"

"According to the parents, these are the people Greg spent the most time with. We've got a Cole and David Young. Frank Hernandez. Alan Woodward. And there are more, but those four are at the top of his list."

I nodded. The circles might only have Alan Woodward in common, but in a town the size of Cleveland, it seemed unlikely the young men wouldn't have known one another, if only through high school, of which there are three.

"Any of them seem promising?" I asked.

"David Young seems like the path of least resistance to me, wouldn't you say?"

She looked at TJ again, who nodded and said, "It's going to be tricky, though, seeing as how he died from a drug overdose about five months after Greg went missing. But he was married, so I'm sure we can track the wife and brother down easy enough. Woodward is happy to chat. That just leaves Frank Hernandez."

"Right," I said, making a note of the names. "Well, for now, let's put Hernandez on the back burner. We know Woodward appears to be helpful but, as Ronnie used to say, trust but verify. Young's wife, though. Having lost her husband to drugs, she may have an ax to grind. I'd look to her next. Maybe she knows something, maybe she doesn't, but you should be able to get a read on her and then go from there. And, while you two do that, I think I'll set up a lunch meeting of my own. Maybe it's time we cast a wider net."

They nodded, stood up and walked out of the office, leaving me alone once more with my thoughts.

I hesitated for a moment, then took my cell phone from my pocket.

I didn't know if Kate could help or not, but I knew I could depend on her to see things from a different perspective.

I asked her to meet me at the Warehouse on Riverside, then headed back to Tim's office to give him the names, walked out to the car, and drove across town feeling... antsy, is the only word I can think of.

22

Thursday afternoon, 12:40pm

THE WAREHOUSE ON RIVERSIDE IS LESS THAN FIVE
minutes away from the Chattanooga Police Department, so I
wasn't surprised to find Kate waiting for me when I arrived. It
was, and has been for as long as I can remember, one of the most
popular lunch spots in the city. And it had outdoor seating,
which meant Samson could join us. I love that big hairy dog,
and I think he likes me too.

I stepped through the small gate and pulled out one of the
wrought iron chairs, reaching down to scratch the dog behind
his ears. He grinned at me, showing his teeth as he wagged his
tail. It's a terrifying sight if you don't know him, especially as he
was wearing his K-9 officer's harness and badge. His K-9 status
is as an honoree, but he wears it proudly and has proved his
worth, even taking a bullet in the line of duty, bless him.

He gave the back of my hand a lick, then settled down with his
chin resting on his forepaws, keeping an eye on the area. Dogs
are curious enough to begin with; police dogs are never off-duty,

and Samson was no exception, even if his official capacity was somewhat... gray.

"You must be up against a wall," Kate said, setting her menu aside and looking across the table at me.

"No hello?" I asked. "No how's the weather?"

She held out her hands, looked up at the sky and said, "It's April in Tennessee and it's not raining. I'd say we can't really ask for anything more. So let's hear it."

"Fair enough. Does the name Detective Louise Baker ring any bells?" I knew it was an incredibly vague way to place it, but I'd found, with Kate especially, it was better to just leave things open as opposed to lead her down one path or another.

"Maybe," she said after a moment. The waiter came by and took our orders, buying her a little more time, and then she took up the conversation again. "The one I'm thinking of isn't from around here, though. Am I on the right track?"

"She used to be out of Cleveland. Now she's humping through the snow in Anchorage."

Kate nodded. "Yep. I know her. What do you want to know about her?"

With anyone else, even another police officer, I would've been surprised, maybe even suspicious, at the almost instant recognition. But Kate was something else entirely. Her mind grabs onto information and locks it away in some kind of internal storage unit to which only she has access, never knowing when she might need it again. I shudder to think of the stories she could tell about me.

"Well, for starters, why is she such a pain in my ass?" I asked.

Kate laughed. "I think the question there is, why is everyone such a nuisance to you?"

"Hey." I held up my hands. "I'm a loving family man now. And I talk to you."

"Yeah, yeah." She grinned. "Me and the rest of your team are tools in the toolbox. But I get it."

I thought about what she said for a moment. Surely that wasn't how I portrayed myself. But before I could respond, she had started again.

"The Alaska thing is what jogged my memory. There was a little hush-hush rumoring going on when she took off, but honestly, I didn't pay enough attention to it to tell you one way or the other if it was believable or not, but I'll look into it."

"Thanks, Kate," I said. It was such a relief to have someone on the inside, someone who knew what I needed but never questioned the why.

Kate and I had always worked well together professionally, though for some reason, that dynamic hadn't carried over so well when we'd tried it on a personal level.

"Anything else?"

I sighed. "Maybe, maybe not. This is more one of those situations where I just want your take on things; makes me feel like I'm not going about this half-cocked."

"Shoot," she said, smiling.

I gave her the rundown of what had been going on with the case so far, explaining how, if I needed to, I had no problem going to visit Detective Baker on my own dime and dragging the truth out of her. It wasn't the trip to Alaska that I was so concerned about; but that, if I went soon (and sooner in these cases is almost always better than later), I'd likely not be around for the exhumation of the bodies. I hadn't heard anything certain one way or the other, but my feeling was that once the dominos started falling in that direction, it wouldn't be a process anyone wanted to drag out any longer than necessary.

"Of course there's the other thing to consider," Kate said, taking a sip of her drink.

I frowned. "Go on."

"It's cold in Alaska. It's just barely starting to think about being warm here. Do you really want to go chasing some woman around Anchorage?"

I laughed. "I'd prefer she'd gone to Miami, that's for sure, but..." I held out my hands.

"Nah." Kate waved my comment away. "You'd lose your mind in Miami. The laid-back north, that's more your style. The laid-back, frostbite-inducing, stay-out-of-people's-business north."

"You have a point," I said. "But if it comes down to it, I don't want to miss my chance. We've only talked twice, and I don't know what has her spooked, but it's something. The last thing I want is to get up there and find out she's jumped across the strait to Russia."

"I wouldn't worry about that." Kate laughed. "But I get your point. You want to know what I would do?" Then, before I could answer, "Of course you do, or you wouldn't have asked me here." She wiped her fingers on a napkin and looked across the table at me. "Right now, you've got two things to consider; one you can make happen on your own, the other you have to wait for. I think that's what's really bothering you, Harry. You don't want to have to wait because, whether it's accurate or not, you feel like you're wasting time."

I looked down, shaking my head. "How much do I owe you for this impromptu therapy session?"

"Just lunch." She smiled. "If I were you, I'd sit tight. I know that's not your strong suit, but it's better than getting halfway to Anchorage and finding out they're going to start the exhumation without you."

"All right," I conceded. "You've got a point. But since you're rattling off all these nuggets of wisdom, what do you suggest I do in the meantime? And don't forget, if Baker can lead me to the ME's report, then we may not need the exhumation at all."

"That's a big if," she said. "And you're also getting that hyper-focus you always do. Maybe Detective Baker can lead you to it, sure. But maybe someone else could, or maybe a strong wind will blow it in through your office window."

I cocked my head a little, then said, "Are you going where I think you're going?"

"Officially," she said, "I'm not going anywhere. What I'm saying is that there are more ways to approach a problem than you sometimes seem to see. You get an idea stuck in your head and you hammer on it till it works. And most times, that's fine. But don't lose focus on your other options. You need to find a file that was more than likely entered into a computer some-where in a large database for a small-town police station. I'm no computer genius, but I would imagine the PD in Cleve-land, Tennessee, isn't operating on the same level as, say, the CIA."

"You're suggesting... Tim?" I asked.

She held up her hands. "I'm not suggesting anything. All I'm saying is you have options to consider. And what that boy is doing still working for you, I don't know. He should be working for the NSA."

"I appreciate him and pay him well, is why," I replied.

I leaned back in my chair. Nine times out of ten, Kate was a by-the-book cop, and when she wasn't, it was either because she had to be or because she knew that it was the only way to get things done. Having my employee hack into a police database didn't sound exactly appealing. It sounded likely felonious, to be honest. But he'd done worse, and at the same time, I could understand Kate's argument. The files were supposed to be there for those who were attempting to solve the cases. The chief himself had attempted to give me the file. If I could get someone in there to dig around through the electronic files and see where the information had been misplaced—or hidden—then I was just pursuing a track that would've needed to be done at some point anyway.

"Convinced yourself yet?" Kate asked.

"Just about," I said. "I think the idea sounds a lot worse than it is."

"True," she admitted. "It doesn't sound good. But neither does your case. Something made Detective Baker run and get as far away from Cleveland as she could. Someone is hiding something. If you do nothing, everything stays the same. If you pull the right thread, the whole thing unravels. And you may not even have to pull that hard."

"Because just poking around might draw the right attention," I finished.

"'Right' is probably a tricky word here, but yes. You want answers. So you shake the tree. If nothing else, it'll give you something to focus on without flying across the continent."

I nodded. "I like the way you think, Kate."

She nodded, sucked on her bottom lip, and said, "I'll have the crème brulée, please."

"Woof," Samson said.

23

Thursday afternoon, late

Considering that Heather and TJ had a full afternoon of interviews, I wasn't in much of a mood to hang around the office any longer than I had to. I set Tim to work on poking around with, as I should've expected, very little coaxing needed. The kid looks at cyber security the way most people look at a sudoku puzzle; it's a clever little game for him to try and figure out. Fortunately for the folks with the Sunday paper on their knee, sudoku can be solved without any criminal charges being threatened. I tried to make it clear this was a criminal matter and that just leaving a trace of his presence could be enough to put us all in jail. Having said that, I knew that searching the Cleveland PD databases without leaving a trace was part of the game. Tim would be in and out, and no one would be any the wiser.

So I spent the rest of the afternoon trying to think of anything other than the case at hand. Kate had given me some solid advice, even if it was a little easier said than done.

I debated calling Doc Sheddon to see what the situation was with the exhumation, but given the number of hoops he'd have to jump through to justify his request, I didn't think pestering him would hurry the process along any. We'd received permission from both Jacob Harper and Blake McDaniel. Now it was just a matter of Doc working his magic to get approval.

I tried poking my head in Jacque's office for a few minutes, but she had a solid stack of files on either side of her desk and, with a dour flip of an eyebrow, reminded me I could probably find some mundane but necessary work, rather than let it trickle down as I'm prone to do.

It's not often I find myself watching the clock and waiting for the day to end. True, there were more than a dozen mundane cases that probably could have used my attention; there's always plenty going on in a town the size of Chattanooga. But none of them held my attention. It was an exercise in guts that kept me there till five. I knew if I left early, though, I'd just spend the downtime bugging Amanda, or maybe even my father. Not that he would have minded; I rarely see anything of him these days.

And so, at the stroke of five, and not a second after, I hit the parking lot and headed home. Amanda was more than pleased to see me pull in on time for once, though she had her hands full with a fussy Jade and, despite my skills in getting the little girl wound up, I wasn't known for my ability to soothe her when necessary.

It was too cold for a swim, so I grabbed my sneakers out of the closet and slipped into some gym shorts, figuring a run might be just the thing to give my girls a little time to settle down and me a chance to burn off some steam.

My jaunts around the neighborhood are never too predictable. It's more a situation of wanting to see what I can see, a born curiosity that leads me where I go. The fact that it makes me hard to pin down and ruins any last-ditch attempt at plotting my schedule doesn't hurt either. Most days, I can tell roughly by how I feel what my pace will be and go wherever my whim decides to take me. The less I have to think about, the better.

I'd started out going south on East Brow Road, made two rights onto West Brow Road, made the turn onto Point Park Road and back onto the north end of East Brow and started back home past the Battles for Chattanooga Museum and happened to glance at my reflection in the plate glass windows when I realized something.

Coming up on an intersection, I made a right onto Lyerly, picked up the pace and sprinted to the end of the block and made a left onto the one-way section of West Brow, then dodged behind a tree and waited.

Sure enough, not thirty seconds later, I saw it. A strangely familiar blue SUV. If I had any previous doubts, the speed told me everything I needed to know. It cruised slowly to the end of Lyerly, slowed to a stop, then made a slow right turn onto West Brow going north. I waited until the car reached the next intersection, then stepped out from behind the tree.

I'd already made a mental note of the license plate number, so I hit the button on my phone, killed the music I'd been listening to and stepped off the curb.

Without a clue on where to go, the SUV was idling at the stop sign. I could almost hear the driver cursing himself. Losing a mark on foot is easier than most people think, but based on what I'd seen so far, this guy wasn't exactly an expert tail. I jogged up the opposite side of the street, wishing for once that there had been more traffic, some parked cars, anything I could duck down behind. My best shot now was staying out of his mirrors and in his blind spot until I could get closer.

The brake lights flashed and I knew I was losing my chance. Throwing caution to the wind, I cut back into the street and sprinted after the vehicle.

I was within a few paces when the driver must have spotted me because, with a squeal of the tires, he hit the gas and the SUV made a sharp turn onto Point Park Road.

I stopped running, knowing there was no way I could catch him on foot, and watched as the SUV tore along the block and made a screeching turn onto East Brow.

I took my phone out of its strap on my bicep, tapped in the number and sent it to Kate and asked her to run it.

It would take her at least a few minutes and my mind was already in top gear, trying to figure out the best plan for a guy more than a mile from home and with nothing but his own two feet to get him there.

I figured I was the one being followed, the only one being followed. Jacque would surely have noticed something, and so would Heather.

I turned toward home, the adrenaline pushing me on. The odds were that someone had been watching the house. The question was, from where?

I ran to the end of the block, made a right, and headed home, dodging the pedestrians gathered around the museum and the park entrance, all the while the thoughts churning inside my head.

A tail in Cleveland was one thing. A tail on my home turf was a different thing entirely. The only thing I was sure of was that the trip to Alaska was off. They might be willing to follow me thirty minutes down the highway, but across the country was another story. If I skipped town, it would cool things down for me, but for Amanda, Jade, and Maria? Well, it didn't bear thinking about. Detective Baker could have this round; I wasn't leaving those important to me on their own.

I was at the gates to my home when I felt my phone buzz on my arm. I stepped through into the driveway, sweaty, breathless, and with one eye on the phone screen and another in the front room where I'd left Amanda.

The living room was empty, but I could hear voices from the kitchen, the reassuring chatter of Amanda and Maria. I figured Jade must've settled down enough to catch a few winks before dinner or keep herself otherwise occupied. I dashed into the house, closing the electronic gate behind me, and hurried along the hall, scanning the text from Kate as I went. Just before I stepped into the kitchen, I stopped, looking at the name on the screen.

"Frank Hernandez. Cleveland, TN. I can get more if you need it."

Frank Hernandez? It was one of the names on Sneed's list. I'd have to get in touch with TJ and Heather ASAP, but first, I needed to take care of things on the homefront.

I glanced up just as Amanda paused at the end of the hall. Her look of surprise at seeing me there and looking so... drained was replaced by one of concern.

"What is it?" she asked. "What's wrong?"

I took a breath, as much to settle my nerves as to slow my heart rate. Besides, the last thing I wanted to do was to make this out to be more than it potentially was. "I want to talk to you and Maria for a minute," I said.

"Sure, okay." Amanda turned and walked back into the kitchen and leaned against the counter. Maria stood by the stove, stirring whatever it was she'd decided to cook for our dinner that night.

"The case I've been working on," I began, looking back and forth between them, "it's technically based out of Cleveland, so I don't want you to worry too much over this. Everyone I've talked to, all the people I'm interested in, are almost forty miles away."

Amanda raised an eyebrow, and I could tell what she was thinking.

"I know that's not much," I said, "but I also want you to know this isn't something I foresee being an issue for the two of you. It's more a situation where I need you to keep your eyes peeled as you go through the day." I moved over to the fridge, grabbed a pad of paper we kept stuck to the door for grocery lists and jotted down the license plate number on two sheets, ripping them off and handing one to each of them. "This is the plate number of a dark blue SUV that's been following me and Jacque, and I just caught him following me on my run."

They exchanged a glance, and before it could get too out of hand, I continued. "The guy driving the car isn't a pro, so the fact you're aware should be more than enough."

"Should be?" Amanda asked.

I took another breath, then said, "I can tell you this. When he realized I'd made him, he tore off down the road like a bat out of hell and is probably back to Cleveland by now. Whatever he's doing, I think he's just watching. But..." I looked at them each in turn. "I don't like to guess about things like this. I've already sent the number to Kate and we've got an ID on him. I know who he is. So, if you see the car, don't screw around. Call me. Call Kate. We want to err on the side of caution, okay?"

Amanda looked at me for a moment, studying my face, my expression, trying to read exactly how concerned she should be. Finally, she looked down at the paper, folded it, tucked it in her jeans pocket and said, "Okay."

It wasn't much, but knowing her as well as I do, I knew it was enough. I looked at Maria. "You understand? No heroics. You see this guy, just get ahold of someone as soon as you can. You're not in any danger, but I want to know what it is about me he's so intent on finding out."

"Heroics." Maria laughed. "I do not do heroics. I try my best to stay in control."

You have to understand something about Maria. At the time, she was forty-three and an ex-ATF special agent. She's an expert shot and as tough as a pair of old boots. She's as much a bodyguard as she is a nanny.

She put the paper on the counter next to the sink, and I went over and handed it back to her. "I don't want to make more of this than it is, but please, hang on to this. It might be nothing, but it could be a lot."

"Okay, okay," she said, taking it from me and tucking it into her pocket. "Always it's an adventure with you. Why don't you stay home with your pretty wife? Your daughter? You have a good life here. Go on vacation. Stop chasing killers."

I glanced at Amanda. We were both trying to stifle a laugh. I turned to Maria and said, "If we went on vacation, what would you do without us?"

"Simple." Maria looked at me, a hand on her hip. "I would go, too. What would you do without me?"

I tore a paper towel from the roll by the sink and blotted the sweat from my brow. "You make a good point." I laughed. "And that's why I need you to keep an eye out for this guy. *We*," I emphasized the word, encompassing all three of us, "have plenty to worry about as it is."

"*You*," Maria said, "need to take a shower. Dinner is almost ready."

"Yes, ma'am."

And so I went to our bedroom, knowing that, despite the nonchalance they both had displayed, I had two more very capable and very determined women on my team.

Maybe Frank Hernandez would pick up on that and, if he knew what was good for him, back off.

24

Friday morning, 8am

IF AMANDA AND MARIA WERE WORRIED AT ALL ABOUT THE tail, they certainly didn't show it. Amanda, at least, slept like a log. Unfortunately, the only reason I know that is because I didn't.

The more the loose ends piled up, the more my brain kept playing with them, trying to find a logical solution.

So, the next morning I was up early, as usual. I forewent my morning run in favor of a quick but decent breakfast, wanting to get to the office early.

For once, neither Amanda nor Maria scolded me for the rush. So perhaps the blue SUV wasn't as far from their minds as I'd thought.

I was the first one through the office doors, though I wasn't the first one there. I met Tim at the coffee machine, and judging by the hours he'd been putting in lately and the haggard look on his face, I knew better than to ask him about Frank Hernandez; not at that moment, anyway.

"Am I going to have to fire you just to get you to go home and get some sleep?" I asked, pouring myself a cup.

"You'd never survive without me," he said, a tired smile on his lips. "Besides, I'm crashing hard. Tonight's probably my night."

"As far as I know, you haven't left here in days," I said. "All of the nights are your nights."

He shrugged. "What can I say? The Cleveland PD has a cloud system for most of its documents. You expect me to see that and just go on my merry way? It's like they're begging me to poke around."

"Don't poke too much," I said. "We're a private enterprise here, and Kate's reach only goes so far. In fact, she never came right out and said this was a good idea. She and I are trusting you to not turn this into a debacle."

He laughed. "Harry, this is like..." He thought for a moment. "Like when people put their house key under a doormat. It's so ridiculous nowadays that the only way it would work is because no one else thinks you would really do it. And all I'm doing is lifting the doormat to see if it's there. We're cool. I promise."

I wasn't entirely sure I bought his analogy, but I saw TJ entering the building and wanted to get the results of their interviews as quickly as I could. "All right," I said, patting Tim on the shoulder as I walked by. "But just remember, it's illegal to be a Peeping Tom."

He laughed and headed back to his office. "Who says I want to see what they've got in there?"

"I do," I said. "I've known you far too long to think otherwise. Hey, one more thing. Not now, but when you've got a minute. Did you find anything on Frank Hernandez?"

He waved a hand over his shoulder as he walked away.

Me? I caught TJ's eye as he turned toward his office.

"TJ," I said. "Snag Heather when she gets here and come see me."

He nodded and walked into his space, flicking the light on. Someday, I thought, someday, I would get the man to have a conversation.

No more than five minutes later, the two of them were back in their respective chairs in my office, ready to fill me in on what had happened with Mrs. Young and Mr. Woodward, round two. TJ didn't look any more excited or disappointed than before, but Heather had a somewhat concerned expression on her face and an air of uncertainty about her, which, for her, was more than a little unusual.

We were about to get started when Jacque poked her head inside. I waved her in.

"I didn't want to miss this," she said, taking a seat by the window. "When you get this many people talking, one of them is bound to say something interesting."

I wasn't sure if she meant Heather, TJ, and me, or the interviews, but I figured it was appropriate either way, so I looked back at Heather and nodded for her to go ahead.

"Well," she started, taking out her notebook and flipping through the pages, "we're kind of getting into uncertain territory here. You want Woodward or Young first?"

"Either or," I said.

"All right. We'll start with the Youngs, then. For the most part, they're pretty cut-and-dried. We already know David overdosed a few months after Greg Sneed went missing."

"We do?" Jacque shot me a glance.

"I was going to fill you in," Heather said. "Now you know."

Jacque tilted her head and raised her eyebrows, then crossed her legs and folded her arms.

"David's wife," Heather continued, "didn't give us much. She said she was suspicious of what he'd been up to, but she'd gotten the feeling it was better she didn't look too deep into it. He'd been on and off drugs since just after they'd met, long stints of sobriety, then spells when he fell off the wagon. She wasn't surprised by the names we tossed out. She said they were people she'd tried to keep him away from."

"People, places, and things," I heard TJ say, more to himself than to us.

"But she was in a bind," Heather continued. "A lot of money was coming in, and everybody can use that, but it was going out pretty quickly, too."

"Dipping into his own supply?" Jacque said.

Heather glanced at her. "That would be my guess. The Sneeds were under the impression their son was dealing but not using. I'm thinking David Young had a similar setup initially. He was just in it to sell, but the temptation got to be too much. Again though, that's just speculation. An OD is always a tricky thing, especially when it comes to a habitual user. Going on and off a substance like he did can cause all kinds of problems, the least of which being the addict's assumptions about his own tolerance. Whatever the case, I don't think we've got anything left coming to us from that angle and, just to be frank, I'd feel bad bringing it up with her again. I know we see a lot of bad situations, but as far as I can tell, this one is as true on the surface as it is underneath. She's just a grieving widow still trying to get her life back together."

I nodded. Heather could read a room at a glance and very rarely had I seen her make a mistake. "What about the other Young? The brother."

"Cole? Ah, yes," Heather said, flipping through her pages.

"He's locked up," TJ said, his voice gruff. "Felony drug charges. He hasn't been around for a good long while, but we can go have a chat with him as well if you'd like."

"I'll keep that in mind," I said. "But you guys have had lock-up detail for a while now. And there may be something else I need you for."

TJ shrugged. "All right."

Heather looked over the desk at me.

"I'll get to it in a second," I said. "We know where to find Cole if we need to. Keep going. What about Woodward?"

"Woodward was a surprise," she said, clearly choosing her words carefully. "Something's going on with him. We could barely get the guy to shut up the first go around, but this time..." She shook her head. "This time, when we told him who we were looking into, he clammed up, tight as a duck's... He didn't have much to say."

"And?" I said.

"Well, basically all he really had to say was that the names we mentioned were," she said, making air quotes with her fingers, "'bad dudes.'"

Jacque snorted a laugh. "Who does he think we usually deal with?"

Heather shrugged. "As I said, either something's happened, or someone's got to him. He was more than forthcoming when TJ and I talked to him before, but this time it was different. He all but asked us to stop looking into them."

"Which, of course, you did," I said.

"Course," TJ muttered.

"And there's more," Heather said. "Woodward claims most of these guys are low-level criminals, and it's worth noting that this is the first time he actually described anyone as being 'criminal.' Dillon and Brian 'raised hell' or 'got into a little trouble now and then,' but he never spoke of them like he did these guys. Whatever they're up to, he didn't want any part of it. Said he didn't want to be a snitch."

"Interesting," I said. "What else?"

"He seemed worried about something," Heather replied. "I think there's more going on here than we thought. Hernandez, the Youngs, Greg Sneed, they're working for someone. At first, Woodward just clammed up when I asked him who it was. But when TJ got up and took a step toward him... then he opened up a little, claims he doesn't know who it is, just someone who goes by the name Sparky."

"Oh Lord," Jacque sighed. "That could mean anything."

Heather nodded. "Exactly. Whoever it refers to, though, that's where Woodward drew the line."

I steepled my fingers, thought for a moment, then said, "Frank Hernandez. What about him?" But before either one of them could answer, I turned to Jacque. "You remember our friend in the blue SUV?"

"That's him?"

"That's him," I said, filling TJ and Heather in about what had happened in Cleveland the day before and the tail we picked up, then continued, "He was up the mountain dogging me on my run last night, so we seem to have hit someone's sore spot. I have his plate numbers and I'll text them to you, but stay sharp."

My phone buzzed, and while I'd usually set it aside while I was in a meeting, the name on the screen caught my attention.

"Hang on," I said. "We may have something else going on here. Everybody sit tight while I take this."

I swiped my finger across the screen and answered. "What's the good news, Doc?"

"Good news indeed," the man said. "And urgent as well. The exhumation is a go. Once we got permission from both Jacob Harper and Blake McDaniel, the approval to proceed came through."

"Good," I said. "When are you wanting to get started?"

"Oh, it's already started," he said. "They're doing it now."

"What?"

"I'll be sure and let you know my findings, but I thought you'd be glad to know you won't be waiting long."

"Thanks for letting me know, Doc," I said. "I appreciate the call."

I hung up and looked around the room.

"Apparently, that ME's report just became a little less important. They're exhuming the bodies now."

"How long till we know something?" Jacque asked.

I shrugged. "However long it takes, I suppose. In the meantime, let's keep up the momentum. Here's the plan for today..."

25

Friday morning, 10:30am

I'D SENT HEATHER AND JACQUE OFF EARLY TO TALK TO Cole Young in Riverbend state pen in Nashville. Getting an appointment for eleven-thirty that morning was easy enough, and they had plenty of time to get there, bearing in mind Nashville is an hour behind us. And while I didn't feel too happy about tacking yet another day of prison time onto Heather's workaday sentence, I hoped that, with Jacque along for the ride, it might be a little more enjoyable than the long silences TJ usually brought to the table. Besides, if he was planning on keeping up his intimidatingly stoic demeanor, I figured I might as well put it to good use. Anyway, they were on the road by just after nine that morning.

I sent a text to Tim on the off-chance he needed any of us and then another to Kate, letting her know where we were headed. It wasn't that I felt like I had to bring her in the loop, but I knew she'd be curious and, to be honest, something about another visit to Cleveland was already feeling decidedly off.

Maybe it was the fact that we were about to elevate the investigation to the confrontation level—by visiting Frank Hernandez —or maybe it was just the knowledge that we had so little to go on. Either way, I'd be glad when TJ climbed into the car beside me. Everyone on the team can hold their own when it comes down to it, but TJ has a certain air about him that says much more without words than any of us ever could say with them. That said, the man is a cold-blooded killing machine. I strapped on my CZ Shadow and we left the office.

As we headed along the highway, he turned to me and said, "You think it's a setup." It was a statement rather than a question. But what got me was how exactly he'd expressed my thoughts.

"Maybe," I said. "I don't know how it could be, but it doesn't feel right. Not at all."

"Hinky," he said, looking out the windshield.

I nodded. "Something like that."

For TJ, this was apparently enough on that particular topic, and we rode in silence the rest of the way to Cleveland.

Everyone on my team has their strengths and weaknesses, and I was surprised to realize that, as much as Jacque and I bat ideas back and forth, sometimes having someone like TJ who was content to just wait and see what happened was the better option. I found it somehow... settling. The only other comment he made was just as we pulled off the highway at Exit 25.

"Pull in there if you don't mind."

I glanced ahead, surprised to see he was pointing at a McDonald's. "Doesn't really seem your style."

He shrugged. "Busy this morning."

I pulled into a parking spot and waited while he ran inside. What he could've possibly been doing that kept him from breakfast was beyond me, but I did know he despised drive-throughs, cell phones, and email. He wanted to see the person he was talking to. I got out of the car, more to stretch my legs than anything else, wanting to run through the potential plan of action for the day one more time before we got down to brass tacks. Just as TJ walked back out of the breezeway, I heard someone call my name.

I saw TJ glance over in the direction of the voice and then back to me. A dark-haired woman was scurrying across the lot from where she'd clearly hastily parked her car. The vehicle was crosswise on the lines and the door was still open.

"Mr. Starke!" she huffed. She seemed very anxious about something. "I can't believe I saw you here," she said. "I've been trying to figure out a good way to get in touch with you without raising any suspicions."

I glanced briefly at TJ, and I could tell he was thinking the same thing I was. *If you need to find me without raising suspicion, then I'm already suspicious.*

As she approached, I suddenly realized I knew who this woman was.

"You've been trying to find some reports," she said hurriedly, glancing back over her shoulder as if she was worried she'd been followed. "The medical examiner's findings. I know where to get them."

"All right," I said, my own nerves now on edge, thanks to her demeanor, constant glances over her shoulder and rapid speech. "Where can I find them?"

"Right here," she said, giving TJ a quick look, but apparently figuring if he was with me, he was okay. "Meet me back here." She looked at her watch. "At... half past twelve. I should be able to slip out then. I'll only have a moment, though, so don't be late. And whatever you do, don't follow me or let anyone see us together."

I started to respond, but she was already rushing back to her car. She jumped in behind the wheel, slammed the door, and tore out of the lot onto Clingan Ridge Drive behind the restaurant as if the devil was after her. And then I had an awful thought: *Maybe he is.*

I turned to TJ. He was standing by the car door, taking a sip of his orange juice.

"That was easy," he said.

"She's..." I searched my memory for her name, realizing that maybe I hadn't ever actually known it. "She works for Wickam. The receptionist at his office. Jacque and I crossed paths with her last time we were in town."

He nodded. "Looks like she's decided to be helpful."

"But she doesn't want anyone to know," I replied. "What the hell is going on in this town?"

"I'm sure we'll find out," TJ said as he climbed into the car. And suddenly, I was worried about her. Clearly, she thought someone was watching her, but was it the same people who had gotten to Polaski? Had she gotten word from Detective Baker in Alaska? Word travels, like I'd been told last time I was in town, but this didn't feel like that. Something was off.

Word was traveling but also being quashed, quietly and efficiently.

I climbed into the car and started the engine. "What do you make of it, TJ?"

TJ shrugged, taking a bite of his sausage, egg and cheese biscuit.

He chewed in stoic silence for a moment, then seemed to make up his mind.

"I don't know, Harry. But time will tell. Seems to me the only thing we need to do now is fill in some time. Let's go see Hernandez and be back here in plenty of time for the meeting. It's easy enough to see the woman's scared out of her mind. Let's not let her down."

I started to respond but then realized he was right. There were too many potentialities in the situation, too many different causes and effects to try and anticipate any or all of them. Maybe it was TJ's military background, or maybe it was the part of TJ that had allowed him to excel in that particular environment, but he quickly saw our only viable option. Playing the guessing game would have been an exercise in futility. After all, who would've ever guessed we'd get stopped at McDonald's?

I backed the car out of the space and headed toward the address we had for Frank Hernandez.

"I'm still not really sure what I expect here," I said as we drew closer to the Hernandez residence. "But I think he may be a runner. He didn't stick around when I approached him last night, and he hasn't done anything more, that we know about, than keep tabs on us."

TJ wadded up his trash and stuck it in the bag. "I guess I should've considered that before loading up, huh?"

It was as close to a joke as I figured he would get, but I appreciated the attempt. By loading up, he didn't mean climbing into the car; he meant his weaponry, which usually consisted of a .45 1911, a Heckler & Koch VP9 and a wicked K-bar knife.

"You can be the muscle," I said. "But just look intimidating. You know, the usual."

TJ nodded and looked out the window for the rest of the drive.

When we pulled up, we could see the place already had an air of emptiness about it. Just another trailer on a sliver of land at the edge of town. The grass needed to be mowed but hadn't yet gone to seed. A small gray corrugated tool shed was off to one side. The curtains looked to be of the type you could buy from a tent at the county fair. A Confederate flag, peace signs, pot leaves, and unkempt bushes were, unfortunately, obscuring the views of either side.

I mounted the rickety steps to the door and knocked while TJ meandered slowly around the edge of the manufactured home, ostensibly looking at nothing in particular while keeping an eye open for anyone trying to shimmy out a back window. After waiting a minute or so, I opened the screen door and beat on the hollow aluminum door.

"Mr. Hernandez," I called, once again feeling the emptiness of the place. "It's Harry Starke. I know you've been keeping an eye on me, so I figured I'd make it easier for you. Open the door. I'm not looking for trouble."

I paused, listening for sounds inside the trailer, but there was nothing, not even the babble of a TV or radio. I raised my hand to knock again just as TJ came around from the far side of the trailer.

"We're wasting our time," he said. "If he was here, we'd know. This place is as quiet as a tomb."

A tomb? I hadn't considered that. "You think he might be dead in there?"

Apparently, TJ hadn't thought about the literal implications of his statement either. "Well," he said, after a moment, "if he is, the SUV isn't here. Which means he either dropped it off somewhere or someone took it. Considering the plates were in his name and we have no reason to suspect anything worse than he's off buying milk and eggs, I'm gonna hold off on making a judgment. But my gut is telling me we're not gonna accomplish anything here. Hell, if he's been following you around, he could be out there somewhere watching us now. And that makes me feel uncomfortable."

That thought hadn't crossed my mind either, and now that it had, I too felt decidedly uncomfortable.

And I hate it when a plan goes awry. It was another strong reminder that I couldn't plan ahead too far. The man actually being there was something I'd taken for granted. Or perhaps had counted on, and now we were in a bind.

"You got a work address for him?" TJ asked. "Maybe he's just out doing the grind."

I sighed. "No. That's the trouble. We don't have much on him at all. The plates, this address. That's about it. I don't even know if he has a job, let alone where. He could be anywhere, even lying on the floor in there," I said, eyeing the door.

TJ thought for a second, then started toward the car. "Well, c'mon then. Last couple times you've seen him, it was because he found you. No need to be messing up the system now."

I didn't like the idea of leaving things to chance like that, but TJ was right. The plan for the day had already gone out the window, so maybe it was best to just let it continue on and hope for the best. As I said, maybe Hernandez had been watching us from the start and was waiting for us to lead him to...

"May as well take a little tour of the city," TJ said as I got in the car. "We got time."

We drove around for the better part of an hour and a half, up and down nearly every damn road in Cleveland at least once, some of them more than that. If Hernandez wanted to track us down, he wouldn't have had an easier job. We were practically waving a flag. But as many loops as we made, no matter how many times we lingered at stop signs or pulled off into the street-side parking, no blue SUV made an appearance.

"Kinda weird," TJ said after a long silence as we sat in a Walgreens pharmacy parking lot. "We haven't even seen a similar car, let alone the one we're looking for. I figured there would've been a false start or two by now."

"Hmm," I said without much interest. It was strange, I agreed, but how many blue SUVs there were on the road in Cleveland, I had no idea. Maybe it was just an unpopular color. Or model. Or combination. A siren started to wail in the distance, and perhaps more out of boredom than anything, I turned to see what was coming down the road in front of us.

The traffic signal at the intersection turned red, momentarily causing the police cruiser to slow down before pulling ahead across traffic.

"Well I'll be," I said. "That was Chief Snow."

Before I could even formulate the thought, TJ expressed it. "We better go see what he's after."

I backed the car out of the space and pulled out to the main street. You'd think following emergency vehicles would be easy, but it's almost more dangerous than driving them. People are prepared for the lights and sirens, but the seemingly random civilian car tearing up the road in their wake is something most drivers never think to look for. Even if they do, they assume you're just being opportunistic and aren't too terribly concerned about cutting you off.

Thankfully, Chief Snow only drove about half a mile before he turned right off the road into a corner lot at the end of a long, mostly empty strip mall. Another police cruiser was already on the scene, as well as an ambulance, both with lights flashing. I stayed back twenty or thirty feet, not wanting to get in the way, but Snow had already apparently pegged us. He threw open the cruiser door and started back toward my car, clearly ready to give us more than a little piece of his mind.

I hurriedly stepped out, hands at chest height. "It's just me," I said. "Harry Starke. My partner and I saw you go by and thought you might need some help."

Snow hesitated for a moment and then broke into a smile. "After the help you gave me last time, maybe I should've called you anyway. If I'd known you were in town, maybe I would've."

"What've you got?" I asked, walking over to meet him, TJ keeping pace at my side.

"Female with head trauma," Snow said. "Called in just a few minutes ago." He looked over at one of the EMTs who was kneeling by the body of a woman at the side of the road; a body I was shocked to see looked more than a little familiar.

"Looks like our lunch meeting got canceled," TJ said.

"Seems to happen a lot in this town," I said somberly, looking down at the body of Wickam's receptionist. *Why am I not surprised?* I thought, And then, a little too late, I remembered her name. It was Rachel.

26

Friday, noon

I LOOKED AROUND THE SCENE, REALIZING WHERE WE WERE, then at my watch, realizing the time. TJ was already two steps ahead of me.

"She was going to walk from here," he said, pointing from where her car was parked and then up the street to where we could just see the golden arches about a block away. "She was going to keep her head down, give you the report, and then probably cut back a different way. Not a bad plan."

"Assuming you don't have someone watching you already." I turned to Snow. "What was the report? No, let me guess. Hit and run by a blue SUV?"

The police chief looked at me for a moment, surprised, and then shook his head. "I should've known you'd know already. That's it exactly. Witness said the driver got out for a moment, most likely to check on the woman. Then ran back to the car and took off. Probably panicked."

"No," TJ said. "He was making sure he got what he came for."

Snow started to reply when my cell rang. I reached down and silenced it, wanting to stay focused on the task at hand. "The driver is a man by the name of Frank Hernandez," I said. "I'm almost positive. He's been tailing me ever since I started poking around. We were here looking for him, but he wasn't home. Now we know why."

"Hernandez." Snow was nodding. "I've been hearing that name a lot lately. Nothing solid, but folks sure seem to like pointing the finger at him. Problem is, all it's been is hearsay."

"And still may be," I said. "A man in a blue SUV is hardly definitive. But if you can track him down, I'm sure forensics will be able to tie the car to the body."

Snow nodded. "I'll put out a BOLO for the car," he said, then paused for a moment and said, "Listen, fellas, I don't mean to be ungrateful, but I gotta be honest with you. The way these things are going, I'm not sure I'd be too keen on sticking around if I were you."

TJ glanced back and forth between the chief and me.

"I appreciate the info on Hernandez," Snow said, "and I'll be sure to keep you posted, but as for now..." He shrugged. "I'm half-tempted to call the state boys in. To be frank, this is beginning to look more and more like it's going to get worse before it gets better."

I nodded. "You're not the only one with that feeling."

"Well, with that in mind." Snow looked down at the ground, then back up at me and continued, "So, if it's all the same to you, I'd appreciate it if you boys would make yourself scarce. The last couple times we've seen each other, it's been in similar circumstances. I know you're in the clear, but I don't think you'd be too interested in spending however long the staties decide it takes to convince *them* of that. Not to mention, I'd just as soon not have two more murders on the list."

I looked at TJ. His face was as expressionless as if we were discussing the weather.

"Well, there's not much else for us to do here besides get in the way," I said. "You know how to get ahold of me, and I'll be in touch if anything else comes up on our end."

The chief looked at me and nodded, clipped his radio back on his belt and reached out to shake our hands. "Take it easy, guys," he said. "I'll be in touch as soon as I know something."

I nodded, turned away and walked back to the car, TJ beside me.

"Let's go get some lunch," I said.

27

Friday, afternoon

IT WAS AFTER ONE WHEN WE FINALLY LEFT CLEVELAND
that afternoon. We'd stopped in at the Little Old Fort for lunch
and were headed back to the office. The ride back to Chattanooga was, as usual, quiet, with TJ sitting stoically beside me
until, as we were passing through Ooltewah, my phone rang. It
was Heather.

"Tell me you've got some good news, Heather," I said.

"I take back anything I may've said to make you think I like
these runs to the hoosegow," she said. "This one was a disaster."

"How so?" I asked as I put the phone on speaker.

"Cole Young." I could almost see her shaking her head. "The
man is a mess. He was all over the place. Jacque and I have both
been wracking our brains trying to piece together anything he
told us that might be of use."

"I'm sure you managed to make sense of it, though," I said. "You think he's on drugs?"

"Oh, he has been, that's for sure. But whether or not he is now, I don't know. What I can tell you is we were pushing some hot buttons, and he was more than happy to use all the colorful language he could think of to let us know that. Unfortunately, only about half of what he had to say wasn't the same recycled story you get every time you go to a correctional facility. The system had failed him. This wasn't his fault. He wasn't receiving rehabilitative services. Yadda yadda."

"So nothing too out of the ordinary then?" I sighed, running a hand through my hair.

"Pretty much," Heather continued. "Which is why we're kind of flummoxed by the last bit of his rant."

"He was wrongfully accused, right?" I said, shaking my head and glancing at TJ, who was staring straight ahead.

"No," she said. "According to Cole, his brother David didn't OD. He was murdered."

"Why am I not surprised?" I said.

I actually *was* surprised. Not that David Young might have been murdered, but by how unsurprised I was. Maybe it was the fact that Rachel had been murdered only ninety minutes or so earlier; that and the death of the ME, Dr. Polaski, and probably Greg Sneed, too, plus our two original deaths. There was a lot going on, so it didn't seem outlandish to add one more to the rapidly rising body count.

"You kinda buy it, don't you?" Heather asked.

"I'm not really sure what to think," I replied. "Cleveland is fighting hard to keep its secrets... but, yes, I can buy it."

"Any word on Hernandez?" she asked.

"Yes," I replied, "but I'll save it for when we're all together. But getting back to David Young, what's your gut telling you? Was Cole telling the truth?"

The pause on the other end of the line was long. Heather is usually quick to make decisions, but she's also meticulous in reviewing them before she commits. "Well," she said finally. "Yes, I think he was."

I told her to get back to the office as soon as she could and we'd talk there.

28

Friday afternoon, 4pm

I USUALLY TRY TO END THE DAY ON FRIDAY BY FOUR o'clock, but Heather and Jacque didn't get back until almost four, and I wanted to get their update before the weekend. Tim was still hidden away in his hidey-hole, so it was just the four of us that gathered in the conference room that afternoon.

After some fifteen minutes of back-and-forth talk about nothing at all, the space took on a contemplative silence before we got on with the serious stuff.

Heather and Jacque had almost the same reaction to the collective events of the day as TJ and I had. A burst of surprise followed almost immediately by acceptance.

"A part of me wants to believe it's insane this has stayed quiet so long," Heather said after a moment of silence. "But as you think about it, it becomes a little less hard to swallow."

"Well, that," Jacque said, "and the fact that no one was looking. It's not hard to miss something if you never knew it was there in the first place. It appears we've stirred up a hornet's nest." She swiveled her chair to look at me. "I know I probably don't have to say this, but I just want to make sure we're all on the same page here. Could Chief Snow be behind all this?"

I shook my head. "I'd be lying if I said it hasn't crossed my mind. It almost seems like he'd have to know, doesn't it? But the way this has all played out so far, I just don't see it. If he's involved, he's doing an amazing job of fooling us all."

"Yeah," Jacque said, sounding almost dejected. "That's kind of what I thought, too. But, you know, we have no other suspects, and he's the one who keeps popping up."

I shrugged. I had no answer, and she was right.

"Okay, okay. I get it," she said as she leaned back in her chair, sighing and looking up at the ceiling. "I just can't believe we were that close to having the ME's report, and then we didn't. That's twice now. I mean, I guess it's good to know it's still out there, or at least it was as of this morning, but I'm starting to think we're never going to see it regardless."

"Then you'd be wrong," a voice said from the hallway.

I looked over at the door to see a bedraggled but widely smiling Tim standing there, holding a sheaf of papers above his head.

"It took a little longer than I expected," he said, stepping into the room, barely able to contain his excitement, "but there isn't a system yet that patience and a little ingenuity can't break." He handed out papers as he circled the table. "I give to you, my dear colleagues, the great secret story, the nearly lost and then found death notes, the official report of Brenda Polaski, Medical Examiner."

I looked down at the four sheets of paper, unable to suppress the smile generated not just by the report, but also by the kid's infectious enthusiasm.

"Great work, Tim," I said. "But you look like hell. You need to get some sleep."

"I'll sleep when I'm dead," he said, still smiling as he folded his arms across his chest and took a stand at the far side of the table.

I was leafing through the pages when he spoke up again.

"Before we get carried away here," he said, "I think I should tell you that what you're holding in your hands right now is pretty much based on pure luck."

I glanced up at him, surprised.

"Not on me getting in," he said quickly. "But that there was anything to find at all. Something like this is always bounced around before it finds a home. Sometimes people don't delete their emails. Sometimes people get CC'ed. Sometimes there's a 'reply all' when there's only supposed to be a 'reply.' But this one... this is the only copy I could find. Everything else, even at the periphery of this particular report, it's either encrypted or it's just a ghost."

"Meaning?" TJ asked.

"Like Shakespeare's lost plays," Tim said. "We know they existed because people talk about having seen them. But as for finding a playbook, no dice. This report is the same. It's mentioned in emails it isn't attached to. There are files that tag all the pertinent people involved that have yet to give up their other secrets. The one thing I can tell you for sure is that this isn't a case that just slipped through the cracks and wasn't properly documented. What you've got here is what wasn't properly destroyed."

He put his hands in his pockets, rocking on his heels. Like TJ, Tim wasn't much of a talker, but it was more due to his self-isolation than anything else. "Look through that, though," he said, winding up his speech, "and I think you'll see why."

I only had one thing on my mind as I flipped through the pages quickly, knowing I'd reread it properly at my leisure and compare and contrast it with all the partial, hearsay versions we'd already heard. The tox screen, though, that was hard science.

Jacque was apparently a moment ahead of me, and just before I'd finished reading Dr. Polaski's findings, I heard a low whistle come from the seat across from me.

"If I wasn't reading it, I don't know if I'd believe it," she said. "I mean, these are two young guys with nothing to do but knock back a few beers and raise hell. This reads like they were trying to stay sober."

I glanced at the numbers on the chart. "These aren't even over the legal limit."

"Close," Jacque said, "but that's what I'm saying. If they were hanging out with Woodward beforehand, we're looking at a serious lag between the last drink and the time of death. They'd metabolized almost everything, or anything, they'd drank."

"What about the THC?" Heather spoke up.

"Actually," Tim said, "that's not much better. Think about how long that stays in your system. I mean, sure, it's great for proving use, but it's not so hot when compared to something like alcohol. Usually, that's not a problem, though. If you smoked it, you broke the law. End of story. Doesn't matter when. The alcohol is the one that's tricky. You jump in and out of legality with it. Like an arc. And then you have to prove the person was driving or whatever while they were over the limit. Marijuana, you just snip a bit of hair, see that they smoked at some point in the last month, and that's as good as if you knocked the bong out of their hand."

"Honestly," Jacque said, "even if you'd knocked a bong and a bottle of Jack out of their hands, we'd have what we need to know. There is no way these guys were intoxicated enough to pass out. And especially not so gone as to go to sleep on the railroad tracks."

I was about to respond when my phone buzzed on the table. Seeing Doc Sheddon's name on the screen, I held up a finger and answered it.

"Doc. I'm glad you called. I've got something you're going to want to see," I said.

"What a coincidence," he said. "I was about to tell you the same thing. Exhumation is complete. The autopsy is complete. We're not out of the woods by a long shot, but I'd say we're making progress."

"What did you find?"

The room was silent. We'd all been waiting for this as much as we'd been waiting for the ME's report.

"It was murder. Plain and simple," Doc said. "No two ways about it."

"That's what we were just discussing," I said. "Judging from the tox screen, the only thing these guys could have been arrested for is jaywalking."

"Not to burst your bubble," Doc replied, "but the tox screen really wouldn't have made any difference. These young men were shot to death."

I let out a breath I hadn't known I was holding.

"Tell me," I said.

"Well, as usual, it's difficult to piece together too much. That's typically what we rely on you for. But I can tell you this. Brian McDaniel was most likely killed execution style. One shot to the head. Could've been lucky, and it's difficult to tell after this long, what with decomposition and what have you, but he was shot at close range at a downward angle that suggests he was on his knees."

"And Dillon Harper?"

"Mister Harper appears to have made a run for it. Multiple gunshot wounds. Again, decomposition hampers things a bit here, but bullets don't tend to pass through a body without leaving a mark."

"So they were shot and then dragged onto the tracks to cover it up," I said, almost to myself.

"I don't see any other way it could've happened," Doc replied. "And considering what you told me about the tox screen, I'm assuming there was no mention of bullet wounds."

"None," I replied.

"You're looking at a cover-up, then," Doc said.

"Send me over what you have," I said, tossing the pages onto the table in front of me. "I need to make a phone call. Excellent work, though, Doc. As always. Thank you."

"And, as always, my pleasure," he responded, but I was already reaching to end the call.

I ran through the contacts on my phone, found Chief Snow's number and hit send. He answered almost immediately, but judging by the amount of background noise, things hadn't calmed down much in Cleveland.

"Talk fast," Snow said. "I've got more than a handful going on here."

"I'll make it quick then," I said. "We've got the ME's reports, and we've got the second autopsy reports. Your boys were shot and then placed on the tracks. What we have here is a very dangerous situation."

"I think I've already crossed that line," Snow said. "In fact, seeing as how you're neck deep in this, I'd like to officially request your help. You up for it?"

"You got it," I said.

"Then we need to make short work of this," Snow said.

"You'll see us shortly." I hung up the phone and looked around the table.

"You heard what he said," I began. "Things are probably going to start moving fast, which is good, but it also means we have to be twice as careful. Jacque, I know it's getting late, but if you're up for it, you and I are heading back to Cleveland. The rest of you sit tight and work from here. We'll be in touch. When the files from Doc Sheddon come in, go over them with a fine-tooth comb. I need to know everything that jives and what doesn't with the Polaski report. Even if it seems trivial, make a note of it. I think she was trying to point us in the right direction."

I got up from the table and headed for the door, scrolling through my contacts again with Jacque on my heels.

"Who else do you need to call?" she asked. "I thought we were keeping a tight lid on this one."

"We are," I said. "But Amanda's already privy. And she's going to want to know why I'm not going to be home for dinner tonight."

29

Friday evening, 5:30pm

I had Jacque drive while I made the call to Amanda. The traffic at that time on a Friday afternoon was always horrendous, and it was getting on for six when we finally made it through the city and were heading north on I-75.

"Okay, now what?" Jacque asked when she saw me thumbing through my recent calls.

"Time to start putting pressure on," I said. "I think it's time to talk to Detective Baker again."

"You're lucky you aren't getting charged long-distance rates anymore."

"I'm lucky cops have to keep their phones on," I said. "Anyone else and they'd just turn the thing off so I'd quit harassing them. Louise Baker can either deal with me or face a ringing phone the rest of the day, and I'd just about bet you she knows it."

As I'd suspected, the first two calls rang through to voicemail, but on my third attempt, an exasperated detective answered the call.

"You realize this is harassment, right?"

"Hello to you as well," I said, keeping my tone light. "And it's funny you should mention that. I was just saying the same thing to my partner here. And while we're on the topic of potential crimes, are you ready to talk about hindering a police investigation yet?"

"I've already told you; I don't know anything about what you're asking. That case was years ago. If you want to go play inspector with your friends, I can't stop you. But I can make sure you leave me out of it."

"As much as you may wish that was the case," I said, "I'm afraid you're right back in the middle of it. Now I don't by any means think you're bad at your job; just the opposite, in fact. And I don't think they sent you to Alaska, either. I think you're up there because you wanted out, to get as far away from Cleveland as you possibly could. That, in itself, is a bit of a conundrum, but hey, to each their own, right? What I'm really struggling with here is, how could a detective still be considered active-duty if she had so badly fouled up a crime scene?"

"The world is full of mysteries, I'm afraid," she replied. "Good luck with it."

She was about to hang up; I could tell by the tone of her voice.

"Before you go," I spoke quickly, "I just wanted to ask you one thing." I glanced over at Jacque, who seemed to be enjoying the banter. "Did you just not see the bullet holes in those two kids? Or did you simply think they were unrelated?"

The long silence was almost enough to make me think she had indeed ended the call. But, after a very long pause, she finally spoke up.

"All right," she said, sounding tired. "What do you want to know?"

I put the phone on speaker and set it on the console between us. "Just the truth, Detective Baker. That's what I've been telling you all along."

"Listen," she said, after another pause, "I don't want you to think I'm shifting the blame here. I know what I did and I know how things look, but I wasn't the only one involved. I got in over my head in more ways than I care to tell, and when it came right down to it, the only thing I could think of to do was to just get out of there. Get as far away as I could."

"I'd say you pretty well accomplished that."

"Yeah, well..." She sighed and then cleared her throat. "Okay. If we're gonna do this, we may as well do it all."

"Hold on a sec," I said. Then gestured for Jacque to hand me her phone. I opened the record app and said, "I'm going to record this, Louise."

"Of course you are," she replied. "The first thing you probably ought to know is that you're right. Harper and McDaniel were murdered. Obviously, that's no big leap considering what you've found out already, but what you need to understand is that this isn't something only I knew. Everyone involved knew. We picked up bullet casings at the scene for crying out loud."

"When you say 'everyone'..." I prompted her.

"Everyone involved that I knew of and apparently a number of people I didn't."

"So you, the ME, I assume... And?"

"Me, Doctor Polaski, the chief at the time. Anyone who would've seen the initial reports. Even Judge Valentine seemed privy, though he was surprisingly quiet about it."

"Tell me about Valentine," I said. "That's a new name to me."

"He did a pretty good job of keeping himself out of it. Besides, once the investigation was closed, he didn't have any role to play. Nothing to preside over. That doesn't mean he wasn't aware of what was going on, of course. I just don't know how far that awareness stretched."

"You said you were surprised at how quiet he was about it. The two of you were close?"

The sound of Baker exhaling was slow and exhausted. "Pretty close, I'd say. We were sleeping together at the time."

Jacque looked at me and nodded.

"Like I said," Baker continued, "he never spoke to me specifically about the case, but I got the feeling he knew more than enough to get the attention of whoever was pulling the strings. Once we were found out, I didn't stick around long."

"People talk," I said, trying to be at least mildly supportive. "I can't say I blame you for wanting to get out of Dodge."

"It's not that," she responded. "I was leaving in hopes they wouldn't talk. Not long after we caught the case, I started receiving emails with... personal photos of the judge and me together."

"And the blackmailer wanted you to look the other way on Harper and McDaniel," I said.

"Exactly." She was beginning to sound like someone who'd wanted to get it off her chest for a long time and, regardless of the pain and shame, was finding the experience almost cathartic. "So I cleaned up the mess I'd made and buried the murders; they would make sure the photos stayed between me and whoever was sending them."

"That's a high price to pay," I said.

She laughed, though her tone lacked any humor. "You're right. And if it had just been that, I don't think I would've caved. Or at least, that's what I like to believe about myself. It's always easier to imagine yourself better than you are, I suppose."

"What kept you from coming forward?"

"You come across the name Greg Sneed yet?"

"I have."

"Then there's your answer. Whatever he knew, it was too important to blackmail him over. Or maybe he just wasn't willing to play ball. Like I said, I don't know everything about that. I just know about twenty-four hours after he went missing, or whatever they're saying these days, I got a call letting me know we didn't need to look for him and that his body was buried in a junkyard outside of town."

"That's a pretty clear message," I said, wowed by what I was hearing. We had another body to add to the count.

"Clear enough. Like I said, maybe I would've stayed if it had just been trouble for Valentine and his wife. I mean, it takes two to tango, right? But what happened to Sneed was too much to gamble on. I took the hint and got out of there. Alaska seemed far enough to prove I'd keep my mouth shut."

"These other people that you say knew, or were involved, were they blackmailed as well?" I thought back to all the people we had talked to so far. Surely the parents had told the truth. Even the men on the train. It had been so long that I found it hard to believe they would've kept their silence. Then again, threats often tend to seem less threatening when years have passed.

"If you want my guess, and that's all it is, Mister Starke, I'd say just about everybody you know of either took a bribe or got a call similar to mine. I'm almost positive the conductor and engineer did, though the way bodies are turning up, I imagine those two are lucky to still be alive."

I stared out through the windshield, trying to process the information she'd just given me. The pieces all fit together and, like most riddles, it seemed so obvious once the solution was pointed out. Except, of course, we were only halfway home.

"The person or persons who were blackmailing you," I said. "D'you know who it is?"

She sighed again, apparently her go-to reaction to difficult questions. "That's another one of those things I regret. I like to think if I'd stuck around, I'd have done some digging. But things were escalating fast and to heights I didn't expect. Once I decided to go, I just went. Clean break. It seemed like the safest move."

"Right," I said, barely paying attention to this repetition and her attempts at justification.

"I can tell you this, though," she continued, "and maybe it will help steer you in the right direction. That junkyard where Greg

Sneed's body supposedly is buried, it belongs to a man by the name of Frank Hernandez. You need to talk to him."

I looked at Jacque. The smile on her face would have been more appropriate for a trip to a theme park than a murder investigation, but to be fair, I felt pretty good myself.

"That it?" I asked.

"That's it," she replied. "That's all I know. But listen. If you want to talk again, feel free to call."

"Thank you, Detective Baker," I said. "I'm rather glad to hear that."

30

Friday evening, 7:10pm

I ENDED THE CALL WITH DETECTIVE BAKER AND PLACED one to Chief Snow. I knew it was risky to involve the local PD after what Baker had told me, but I had no other option. As to Chief Snow, from what I'd seen so far, he'd shown himself to be both transparent and willing to help, even down to letting us slip away before the state troopers had shown up.

I told him where the body was buried and he assured me he'd get right on it, as well as on the hunt for Frank Hernandez, and gave me directions to the yard. It was on the opposite side of town from our approach, but Cleveland being the size it is, we were able to make the extra miles in no time flat. And it didn't hurt knowing the police chief would have our back if we got pulled over along the way.

We pulled into the junkyard's dirt parking lot just in time to see three K-9 officers prepping their dogs.

I parked the car, and we walked up to the chain-link fence to watch them work.

"Uh-oh," Jacque said.

"What?" I asked.

She looked up at the sky, holding out a hand, palm up, and said, "It's going to rain."

I looked off to the west. The clouds were dark, gathering, but still far enough away that, with any luck, it might hold off long enough for us to get something done.

"They'll be all right," I said, hoping my false confidence would encourage even me. "They'll find him."

"I don't know, Harry. It's been a long time. And this place isn't exactly a bed of roses. It stinks."

I put my hands in my pockets and watched the dogs spread out over the area. "Look at it this way then. What's one more drop of rain in the big picture? These dogs can sniff out a dead mouse from fifty yards, so it shouldn't be that difficult to find a dead body. Besides, it's been a good day so far, maybe more so for us than Detective Baker. After what she told us, her career in law enforcement is over. But I'd say her conscience is now clear, and that's always a good thing. She'll be okay."

"Grand," Jacque said, her voice heavy with sarcasm. "I'm sure I'll sleep better tonight knowing that. Having said that, she needs to lay low until this is over."

"You made it then," a voice said from behind us. I turned to see Chief Snow walking over to join us, his cruiser parked next to my Range Rover. "Though I imagine you must be discussing something else, considering I just got the news myself."

"Well, don't keep it to yourself," Jacque said, smiling. "What's the word?"

"We tracked down Frank Hernandez. Not a moment too soon, either, I don't think. Picked him up at a gas station on the other side of town. He claims he wasn't getting ready to leave the area, but..." He shrugged. "He had his bags packed and was ready to go. Fortunately, though, I'd spread the word and one of our CIs called in and kept him talking at the pump until the cruisers arrived."

"So what's he had to say?" I asked. "Has anyone spoken with him yet?"

"No. Not yet," Snow replied. "I thought I might give you the honor. After all, he's clearly been interested in you for a while. May as well let the two of you have it. And besides," he said and grinned, "it surely won't hurt to let him stew for a bit."

"As long as he doesn't end up dead by the time we get there," I said.

"If he does, he won't be the only one. I've got three officers at the station solely in his honor."

I nodded. "I guess it's just up to the dogs then. What are you thinking?"

Instead of answering, Snow simply nodded toward the yard where an officer was jogging toward us.

"No way," Jacque breathed.

"There's always a way." Snow beamed. "Best dogs in three counties out there," he said as he walked through the gate to meet the officer.

They chatted briefly for a moment, and then Snow beckoned for us to join them.

"Looks like we got a hit," he said brightly and smiled. "We'll have whatever it is dug up in no time. If you'd like, feel free to head back to the station. I'll keep you posted on events here."

I looked at the two men and then at Jacque and said, "What do you think?"

"Let him stew for a bit," she said. "I'm curious. But we'll be in the car. It's going to rain."

I knew Jacque well enough to know that her fear of the rain was nothing more than a put-on to get us away from Snow and the other officers, so I played along.

"We'll stick around," I said. "It's not every day you get to see the best dogs in three counties do their thing."

Snow nodded. "Suit yourselves. I'll be back shortly."

I watched as he followed the officer back into the wreckage piled high in the junkyard and then walked to the car with Jacque. Once we were safely in the relative privacy of the vehicle, I turned to her. "So, what is it?"

She had a thumbnail between her teeth, not biting it, but just applying a thoughtful pressure. "Honestly, I'm not sure," she said after a moment. "Something feels off to me. I mean, Snow comes off as a stand-up guy, but I keep thinking about what Baker said. 'Everyone's involved,' remember? That covers a lot of possibilities. She didn't even know all the names and she was the lead on this thing. And Snow, I mean, you don't just become police chief out of nowhere. Who's to say he didn't get the job specifically because whoever's behind all this knew he would keep his mouth shut?"

"It's a fair point," I said. "And it's crossed my mind more than once as well. The thing I keep coming back to, though, is how helpful can a guy be before he's not just blowing smoke? Let's say Hernandez is expendable; that gives us two options. One, he doesn't realize he's being sold up the river and keeps his mouth shut. That's possible. Or two, the man behind the curtain is willing to risk being exposed just to keep us guessing. You were here the first time Hernandez started tailing us. Did anything about that scream 'professional' to you?"

She sat for a few moments before sighing and resting her chin on her hand. "No. It didn't. You make a good argument, Harry, I suppose. Maybe I'm just being overly cautious. After all, I mean, maybe Hernandez got the word to go and just ran out of luck when he ran out of gas. Maybe him getting picked up wasn't part of the deal at all. Could just be bad luck. Or maybe he intends for us to have an accident on the way back to the station. Who knows? I'm telling you we need to be extra careful. You carrying?"

I nodded. "Aren't I always? Look, I'm never going to fault you for playing devil's advocate, but there is one thing we need to consider, and it's what you just mentioned a moment ago."

"Baker," she said.

"Exactly. Maybe, whatever this conspiracy turns out to be, we'll find that Baker's still on the take and got the call to finally crack, to lead us here. Maybe it's a wild goose chase. But then again, for all Snow knew, we would've hightailed it back to the station, and at his suggestion."

"A lot of branches on this tree," Jacque said thoughtfully.

"Occam's razor," I said. "The simplest explanation is usually the best one. Right now, we've got a suspect in the can and dogs on the ground. I say we let this play out and then do like we always do. Act based on the best information we have."

It took almost twenty minutes to get that next piece of information, but the smile on Snow's face as he walked up to the car let us know it was good news. I stepped out and met him by the hood, taking the small plastic-bagged object he held out to me.

"We tried not to disturb the scene too much," he said, "but I knew you'd want to know as soon as possible."

Jacque leaned over beside me, looking at my hands.

"That's Greg Sneed's wallet," Snow said. "Nothing much more than bones and the soles of his shoes, but if you open that carefully enough, you'll see a driver's license inside. Either whoever put him there isn't the brightest bulb in the chandelier, or they just didn't care."

I handed the bag back to Snow. "The name David Valentine mean anything to you, Chief?"

"The judge?" he said, looking surprised. "Well, of course. Everybody knows Judge Valentine. Why?"

I looked over at Jacque, knowing she had just assessed every tic in the man's reaction.

"I'll tell you later when I know more," I said. "For now, I'd like to go talk to our suspect."

31

Friday evening, 7:45pm

THERE'S SOMETHING ABOUT A PERP IN AN INTERROGATION room that never changes. It's always the same lounged posture, the same irritated, cocky expression. It's as if they want you to know from the moment you walk in they think you're wasting their time and yours. The interesting thing about it is it's only the guilty ones who act that way. It's almost as if they've decided that projecting their disregard for the situation will somehow cow you into screwing up. The funny thing is, though, the reaction of most interrogating officers is the complete opposite. The more respect you give, the more you're entitled to. And vice versa. For some reason, though, none of them, at least those I've interrogated, have ever managed to figure it out.

I watched Frank Hernandez through the glass for a few minutes, running through my questions and his likely responses.

"Oooooh, he's a tough one," Jacque said sarcastically. "How're you going to handle it, Harry?"

I shrugged. "He doesn't want me to waste his time, so I won't. Keep an eye on him from here."

She folded her arms and leaned against the frame of the one-way mirror as I entered the room.

Hernandez was trying to take up as much space as possible, another classic—and pointless—move. It was a dominance attempt that any beat cop would learn on day one. The more space a person can supposedly claim, the more in control he or she thinks they are. The problem is, once the interrogating officer figures out what's going on, it becomes surprisingly easy to not care. And just like that, the balance is restored.

"I figured I'd save you the trouble of following me all around the state and just give you a chance to say whatever it is you want to say," I told him as I walked in. "No sense in wasting time following me around the block or from town to town, wouldn't you say, Frank?"

He looked at me, a half-smile on his lips, but he didn't reply other than to roll his eyes.

"All right," I said. "Clearly you have more important things to do, so let's make this straight and to the point. I know you killed Greg Sneed. All I need to know is why."

"You want me to just hand it to you like that?" He laughed. "You cops are getting lazier by the minute. Besides, it wouldn't do you any good anyway. As soon as you know, you're a dead man."

"If the guy they send after me is anything like you," I replied, "I like the odds."

"Whatever." He looked away, feigning indifference.

"All right," I said, turning back toward the door. "I guess you can just sit here and see what happens then. I'll figure this out one way or another. You're clearly not smart enough to keep ahead of me out on the streets, so you can sit here in this little room. I give you two days before you think of something worth saying. Three, max. Hopefully, between now and then, nothing unfortunate happens to you."

"You can't threaten me, man. You're a cop," he said warily.

"Actually, I'm not. But that's beside the point. And I'm not threatening you. I don't have to. Bodies have a way of turning up, don't they? You're a threat, and I imagine your boss is thinking 'what's one more'? How many people in this facility are on his payroll, I wonder. It's only a matter of time, Frank. Think Jeffrey Epstein."

He laughed. "You don't know nothing. Fine. You wanna know why I did it? It's your funeral, man."

I shrugged. "I've heard that a time or two. Go ahead. Tell me."

Hernandez leaned forward, his elbows on the table. "It was Sparky. He told me to do it, so I did it. That's all the why there is to it." He leaned back, a smug smile on his face. "You better start picking out flowers, bro."

"Sparky," I said. "That means nothing to me. Does he have a real name? Or is that just a pet name?"

He spat at the floor. "You're the detective. You figure it out."

"You're willing to take the heat for this guy," I said, changing tactics. "I've got you down for the Harper and McDaniel murders as well as Brenda Polaski, the DA's secretary, Rachel Waldon—we have your car on that one—David Young and Greg

Sneed. That's six so far, Frank. You've seen your last day of fresh air."

He laughed, rubbing the back of his neck and looking up at me. "You can't pin them on me. No way anybody'd buy it."

"Why's that? Looks pretty good from where I'm sitting."

"Yeah, if you wanna hang something on a man who didn't do it. Ain't no way I'd ever leave a job needin' that much clean-up. I got self-respect."

I ignored the comment for the moment. Most of the folks who took that kind of attitude had a pretty high opinion of themselves. What I needed was the first part of his statement, and I knew with a little pushing, we'd be off to the races.

"Well, you're right about one thing. The Harper and McDaniel murders were a hot mess, and so were those of Polaski and Waldon, for that matter. It would be a shame to pin two murders on you if you didn't commit them and the real killer goes free to live high on the hog while you languish in Riverside for the rest of your days, wouldn't you say?"

The look in his eyes was all I needed to know. I'd struck the right nerve. No matter how much people like to play tough, there's always a clear moment of realization when they see not only are they in serious trouble, but that it was their own self-perceived cleverness that put them there.

"Look, I'm not saying I killed anybody, man," he said.

"Actually, yes," I said. "That's exactly what you're saying. I don't know what you think you know about semantics and linguistics and all the other verbal voodoo nonsense they tell you about loopholes in the law, but we're in Tennessee, Frank. Our juries use common sense. You don't stand a chance. Come clean and maybe they'll take it a little easier on you."

"No, listen to me, man. It's not like that. Look, I didn't kill those two, all right? I didn't. Maybe you can..." He paused, leaned forward again, and continued, "What about this? Maybe I can help you out some and you can let some people know, ya know? Tell the cops I cooperated. That kind of shit, er, stuff."

"You're asking to make a deal?" I said. "I can't promise you anything, Frank, but I can put a word in for you. But you need to tell me the truth. We still have the death penalty in Tennessee, but I'm sure you know that, right?"

"Okay, okay, man. It's like this. Those two, they were just in the wrong place at the wrong time. Wasn't anything personal. They just saw something they shouldn't have. And Sparky, he couldn't have that. So he had 'em taken out."

"By who?"

"The Young boys. And Sneed. Who else?"

"And Sneed had to be killed because he knew too much now too? I don't know, Frank. You're knocking over a lot of dominoes. You kill the witnesses, then you kill the killers. Who's next?"

"It wasn't like that. Sparky doesn't play that way. Greg had to go because he was fixin' to snitch. Though why he'd take responsibility for a mess like that is beyond me."

"And David Young?" I asked. "He was going to rat out Sparky as well? Sounds like this guy needs to find some better company to keep. If we tack you onto the list, it seems like everyone involved is more than happy to talk about it, and that means you're probably next on his hit list."

The jab struck home. I could see it in his eyes.

"I'm just trying to help, man. You wanted answers, I'm giving 'em. Won't matter long anyway. Because you're right. Sparky's getting tired of taking out his own. Be quicker and easier just to focus on you. I earned my keep. The other three, good riddance."

I folded my arms. "Your info might not be as valuable as I thought. We've got two bodies. Sneed and David Young. Cole's still breathing. At least for the moment."

Frank laughed, and it was a sound I don't hear often, or enjoy at all. "He is? Maybe it's you who needs to check your sources, bud."

I thought about pushing him further, but if it was just a ploy to get me turned around, I didn't feel like wasting my time. "I think I'll do just that," I said. "Don't you go anywhere."

I stepped out of the interrogation room to encounter a hushed dialog between Jacque and Snow. "Did you hear that?"

"He was just telling me," Jacque said, nodding to the police chief.

"Word came in during the overnight. I don't know why I wasn't informed of it immediately."

I leaned back against the door. "So Cole Young is dead, too, then."

"Not quite," Snow said. "Took an awful beating. He's in a medically induced coma."

"They've got men on him, right?" I asked.

"They do," Snow said. "At least, I think they do. I'll make a call and make sure. Keep on him. I'll be back."

I looked over at Jacque, shaking my head. "Cole Young? In maximum security. How are they always one step ahead? I mean, look at the crew this guy put together. They're not exactly Ivy Leaguers."

"Well, we've got the goods on Dillon and Brian, though. That's a start, isn't it?" Jacque said.

"Yes, it's a start," I replied, running my hands through my hair. "But it may just lead us down another dead-end trail. You know as well as I do that all of his guys are just lackeys. They pull triggers. They take a cut of whatever money's tied up in whatever this is. And then, whoever this Sparky is, tosses them when he's done with them. We've got to keep digging."

"Where?" she asked. "We've got the murderers: Sneed, the Youngs and Hernandez, who clearly knows more than he's saying. Why not keep pushing him?"

"I'm going to," I said. "But he's scared, and I'm not sure he even knows who Sparky is. And I have a feeling this thing is bigger than a few Cleveland degenerates."

"Meaning?"

"Meaning you may have been right about some things before. But I'm still pretty sure Snow's not involved."

"Really?" she said, her eyebrows raised. "He did look surprised when you brought up Valentine, didn't he? What are you thinking, Harry?"

"I'm not sure," I said, taking my phone from my pocket. "I need to talk to Tim."

He answered after the first ring, and he sounded surprisingly alert.

"Talk to me, boss."

I gave him the condensed version of what Detective Baker had told us. "I need you to see if you can track down those emails. She doesn't know who it was she was corresponding with. Whoever was giving the warnings was operating anonymously, but they have to be there somewhere, right? I want to know who it was. You've already been into the database; this time, go deeper."

"I'm on it," he said.

"I know you are," I said. "Call me back when you have something."

I tucked the phone away, getting ready to plan my next round of questioning with Hernandez, when Snow came hurrying back along the hall.

"You're not going to believe what I just learned," he said breathlessly.

"Is it good news this time?" Jacque asked.

"Great news," he said. "We got footage off a traffic cam just a few minutes ago. Turns out you can see the medical examiner's lot clear as day. And guess who delivered a box of donuts shortly before you arrived the day Brenda Polaski died?"

I listened in silence as he told me, not believing what I was hearing.

"But the intern said Polaski brought them," I said, stunned.

"No, she said she brought them *in*," Jacque said.

"All right," I said. "Here's what we'll do. I need to talk to Hernandez ag—"

I was interrupted by my phone ringing and, thinking it might be Tim, I took it out and glanced at the screen. "Belay that," I said, holding up a finger. "It's Jacob Harper."

32

Friday evening, 8:45pm

"I TALKED TO ALAN WOODWARD AND WE FIGURED IT OUT. I know who's behind it," Jacob said before I could get a word out.

"I do, too," I said and then, hearing the unmistakable sound of a shotgun racking in the background, added, "Now don't do anything stupid, Jacob. I'm here in town with Chief Snow. Let us handle this."

"Yeah right. Sounds like the thing to do, don't it?" Jacob said, his voice cold, emotionless. "It's something I've said all along. I suppose a lot of what I did as a marine isn't that different from what you're doing now. Figure out who the bad guy is, track him down, eliminate him. Of course, in the corps, they make it easy on you. They don't make you think too much. They just tell you who to kill and you go do it. Simpler in a way."

"There aren't many left," I said. "We've got Frank Hernandez locked up right now, Jacob, and he's talking. He's told us what we need to know about your brother's death, and a lot more. But if you're about to head out on some kind of vigilante justice jag, you should know the men you're after are already in the ground. Frank's given us everything we need to close that case. They're dead."

The small laugh that came over the line wasn't any more encouraging than anything else he'd said. "You're a smart guy, aren't ya?" he said. And then, before I could answer, "Yeah, of course, you are. That's why I came to you in the first place. See, when I came back from the war, I figured I was just gonna settle back into my old routine. Tell some good stories. Maybe get a few free beers out of it. Maybe even get laid." He laughed again. "That's the story they sell you anyway. And you probably would've seen right through that line. But you know what really happens when you come back?"

"I don't, Jacob," I said. "But I can't imagine it's easy."

"No, sir, easy is the one thing it is not. See, you can leave the war behind, but it don't leave you. The doc says I got the PTSD. Says I need to see the shrink. Wants to get me all doped up. And I went along with it for a bit, but you know what? I've been thinking. And you know what I figured out?"

"What's that?" I was trying to keep him talking, hoping I could talk him down. I figured every second he was talking to me was one less second he was out hunting down people who may or may not have been involved.

"I don't think I want to be cured," he said. "The fact is, what's going on here now is the same thing that was going on before I left. Maybe not the same people. After all, like you said, they're dropping like flies. But you and I both know that ain't gonna get it. It's the head of the snake that needs cuttin' off. And I reckon me being over there, seeing what I saw, doing what I did, maybe it's the way for me to come back and right some wrongs. Ain't that something?"

I shook my head. It wasn't really such a bad idea. But we're no longer living in the Wild West.

"You're forgetting one thing, Jacob," I said quietly.

"What's that?"

"There are already people fighting the battle, legally."

"And one hell of a job they're doing, too. Half this town probably knows who killed my brother and they've been laughing at me behind my back. Well, no more laughing. I'm doing it my way from now on; the way I was trained, so stay out of my way, Starke, or you might get hurt. I mean it."

"I know you do, Jacob, and those are the people I'm talking about," I said. "If we'd known about this earlier, I would've been here sooner. You called and hired us, Jacob. You trusted us to do this job. Now it's time to step back and let us finish it."

"Oh yeah..." he said. "Thing is though, I hired you to solve the case, not get us justice. And you done that. Good for you. But the fact is, I finally figured it out as well. So, as far as I can tell, our business is done and over. You did well though, Mr. Starke. And I got plenty of respect for you. Now it's time for you to back off and let me finish it."

"I need to know where you're headed," I said. "This is bigger than you, Jacob. You can't deal with it on your own." I wanted to continue, but the silence on the other end told me he'd already hung up.

Jacque was standing off to my side, her eyes wide, her hands on her hips. She was ready to move, like a dog ready to attack. I just had to give the word. Snow, on the other hand, looked anxious. Maybe Jacob was right. Maybe this was a battle that needed more than just the local PD to handle it. Corruption is like mold. It spreads slowly, but if it isn't checked, it will take over everything, and it's poisonous.

I knew Snow had nothing to do with the case, that he likely stepped up to the chief's position thinking it would give him a nice pension and some easy years before retiring to Florida like every other old lawman. But it wasn't time for him to hang up his badge yet.

"Listen." I turned to Jacque. "He's going to make a move. I don't know what he knows or what he's thinking, so we can only hope he's headed the same place we are." I looked over at Snow. "You need to get your people out there looking for him ASAP. Don't try to take him down unless you absolutely have to. He's a marine. He knows how to fight and kill. Consider him armed and dangerous, so don't push him. If you can find him, you might be able to keep him contained. I don't think he'll go after cops; you're the good guys, after all." I paused. "But don't count on it either. He's got his mind set on doing this thing all by himself, and he isn't likely to stop until someone's dead."

"Who though?" Snow asked. "We know who it is... at least we think we do, but does he know, and if he does, how? Surely you're not bluffing him."

"I'm not bluffing anyone," I said as I brushed past the chief and opened the door to the interrogation room.

Hernandez was back to his previous cocky self, the chair tipped back on two legs and a foot up on the table.

"If you were hoping to pull a deal," I said, "now's the time to do it." I glanced down at my watch. "You got just a few minutes, now spill it."

He smiled and shook his head. "Ain't a deal in the world you could offer me."

"Wickam really must've done a number on you," I said, shaking my head.

And the look of total shock on his face washed away the last vestige of doubt lingering in my mind. "Come on, Hernandez," I said. "You think I wouldn't figure it out? Occam's Razor. It's the simplest solution."

He gave me a look that clearly expressed he had no idea what I was talking about. "Okay," I said, "how about this, 'Eliminate the impossible and whatever remains, however improbable, is the solution,' or something like that. Wickam shot himself in the foot. One, he's been eliminating too many people. You said it yourself, so I'll give you credit for that. But I hope you've followed your own thoughts to their logical conclusions."

"And what might that be?"

"Think about it, Frank," I said. "Wickam, Sparky, whatever you want to call him, he's eliminated a lot of people lately. There are only a few left, Detective Baker, for one. Then he had the balls to deliver the donuts that killed Brenda Polaski himself. Now he's dismantling the tents, and he's not taking anyone with him. You think he's going to come down here, old west style, guns blazing, and bust you out of hold up? No. The day they put you into general population is the day you die. You want to stay alive? You'd better talk."

He shrugged, but I could tell my words were ticking over in his mind.

"If I were you," I continued, "I'd take a good long look at my food. Those donuts Doctor Polaski ate were laced with cyanide."

Not much happens in an interrogation room that surprises me anymore, but what Hernandez did next was pretty low on my list of expectations. He grinned.

"I reckon if that's how it's gonna play out then, my friend, I sure hope he saves some for you."

I stared at him for a moment, not out of shock at his threat but out of pity. Whatever Wickam told these men, whatever they saw him do, somehow, he'd managed to foster an undying loyalty to his cause. I nodded slightly. "I guess we'll see who gets theirs first, then." And I turned and walked out of the room.

As I pulled the door closed behind me, my phone rang again. Jacque and Snow were still standing by in the hallway, both anxious to move but unsure where to go. I held up a finger and answered the call.

33

Friday evening, 9:25pm

"It's Richard Wickam, the DA!" Tim shouted into the phone. "He's the one who threatened Detective Baker."

"Thanks, Tim," I said quietly. "Anything else?"

"That's not enough?" he said, sounding almost hurt.

"It's enough to confirm what we were already thinking. Good work, son. Are you at the office?"

"Where else would I be?"

"Good. Sit tight. I don't know what I'm going to need, but if you get a call from me, don't mess around. Answer it."

"On it."

He ended the call, and I looked back at Jacque and Snow, who was talking into his shoulder mic, sending officers to the Harper residence. "Get a team ready to move on the DA's office and his home as well," I said when he glanced up at me. "We need to cover all the possibilities."

He nodded and added my request to his order while I pulled Jacque toward the door. "We've got about thirty seconds head start on these guys," I said. "Let's not waste them."

We ran out the front doors and across the street to my car, and I had the engine started and in reverse almost before we had the doors closed. And it wasn't a second too soon.

Only minutes later, we pulled up to the DA's office to see a beat-up old pick-up truck parked cockeyed outside the front doors, the driver's door open and the dome light on. I cursed under my breath. "Of all the mistakes people have made in this case," I snapped, "of course Jacob's the one that doesn't miss a beat."

"Look at it this way," Jacque said, climbing out of the car, "at least now you know he's not out jamming a gun in someone else's face. I'll call Snow."

I pulled my Shadow from its holster, checked the mag, racked one into the chamber and tucked the weapon into the waistband of my pants, thinking how reassuring it was to feel its weight there again. "Hang back until I know what's going on," I said and made my way to the front of the building.

It was almost ten that evening when I stepped out of the car and approached the building. The glass in the front door was smashed, from where Jacob had forced his way in, I supposed. With an entry like that, to a place like this, he would have been lucky Wickam didn't shoot him the second he set foot in the building. It might not have been the worst idea, from Wickam's perspective, anyway. An open and shut case of self-defense.

I slipped past the receptionist's desk and down the hall toward the main office. I hadn't gone far when I heard voices. I slowed and crept toward the light spilling out into the hall through an open door. I stayed tight against the opposite wall to give myself a better angle of view into the room.

Two paces more put me in position to see Richard Wickam seated behind his desk, hands up, and Jacob Harper standing by the window, pulling the string on the blinds to close them, his other hand holding a shotgun, waist high, the barrels pointed at the DA. It wouldn't be a precise shot, and the recoil would probably snap his wrist; but with a weapon like that, precision isn't exactly a necessity. Especially not for a man like Jacob Harper.

I watched as he checked the angles on the blinds, obviously ensuring anyone outside would have no more than a guess if they wanted to shoot at him. Then he walked slowly back toward Wickam.

If I was going to make a move, this was the only chance I had. Jacob would be able to see me without losing his visual on Wickam, which would reduce the odds of him firing on instinct or fear. I held my hands out in front of me and called through the door.

"Jacob, it's Harry Starke. I'm on my own and I'm walking in now, all right? Keep the gun on Wickam if you want, or turn it on me, but don't shoot. It's just the three of us."

I stepped slowly into the office, keeping my hands where he could see them but letting them fall slightly as I moved. As far as I knew, Jacob still considered me a friend, so I wasn't too worried that he'd turn the gun on me.

I glanced at Wickam. His hands were flat on the desk in front of him, and the cocky grin on his lips was similar to the one Frank

Hernandez had been sporting only minutes earlier, despite the 12-gauge pointed at his chest.

"You don't need to be here, Mr. Starke," Jacob said, glancing briefly at me before focusing his attention again on Wickam.

It was a promising sign. He didn't see me as a threat. At least not yet anyway. And that was a good thing, for me.

"I know what he did," Jacob said, "and I'm going to fix the problem once and for all."

"And then what?" I said. "Are you planning on shooting me too? Look, Jacob, I've been trying to help you out, and I still am. We have him. We found him. We both did. This is the end of it. He's going down for the rest of his life. We'll hand him over to Snow and walk away."

"Who says Snow isn't in on it?" Jacob asked, glancing at me. "Every time I turn around, I find another so-called friend, another supposed ally, is just tucked away in this man's pocket. I trust me, and I trust this gun. Seems like the simplest solution to me."

"That it might be," I said, taking a few steps farther into the room, trying to get closer to him. "But Snow isn't one of his. I can assure you of that."

"Oh, you think?" Wickam said, smiling. "Trouble is, you never really know, do you? Though in the end," he said and laughed, "what difference would it make? You shoot me and you're going away for life. If you think I'm the tip of the iceberg, well, think again. I'm the one in charge. Let's see what you've got, soldier boy... You know what I think? I think you're just another punk up to his eyes in something that's way over his head, and this is just a little show to help you sleep better at night. You're not going to shoot me; you haven't got the balls."

"Shut up," Jacob said. His voice was quiet, calm. It was the worst possible response I could've hoped for. He was going to do it, regardless of what might happen to him.

"You know he's lying," I said, trying to talk him down, to get him to turn his attention back to me. It was the only shot I had at keeping him from turning Wickam's office into a murder scene. "But you know what? Even if he's not, we need him alive to put this thing to rest. What if he isn't the head of the snake? Come on, Jacob. You chose me. I didn't choose you. This man..." I gestured toward Wickam. "He may think pretty highly of himself, but like all the rest of his kind, he finally fell to the good guys."

Jacob glanced at me, not wanting to pay attention but also fighting his training. It wasn't a perfect parallel, but somewhere in the back of his mind, I think he was seeing me as a superior officer. At least I hoped he was.

"They get cocky," I continued. "And they get caught. We caught him, Jacob. Thanks to you. Surely you don't want to give him the easy way out, do you?"

What happened next was very fast.

From somewhere outside, in the hall, we heard a noise. A thunk, a misplaced shoe hitting the bottom of one of the potted plants. It wasn't much, but it was enough.

Jacob turned, the gun barrel moving with him, away from Wickam. Thankfully, whatever was happening in the hall was much less of my concern than Jacob's.

I kept my eyes on Wickam, who, having no concern other than his own survival, reached down and jerked open the center drawer on his desk.

"Don't do it!" I shouted, my hand already reaching for the pistol in my waistband, even as my body started to move toward Jacob.

Wickam's hands came up above the desk, a snub-nosed revolver clasped between them. But I was faster.

It wasn't the greatest shot I ever made, but at close range, sometimes, it really doesn't matter. Jacob, his attention focused on the hall, only caught my movement out of his peripheral vision, and the explosion from the CZ startled him.

Wickam rocked back in his chair, blood spurting from his shoulder as he cried out in pain. I'd lunged for Jacob with my shoulder as I drew and caught him solidly on his right shoulder, knocking him sideways and the shotgun from his hand.

We both hit the ground hard, but he didn't struggle. Looking back on it, I imagine he thought I'd taken Wickam out for him, and in a different situation, I might have done just that. But execution was never my style.

I held Jacob pinned to the ground as Jacque rushed into the room, her own gun drawn and aimed at the DA.

"He's covered," I heard her say over my shoulder.

"More than you realize," Wickam said, wincing with pain. "You really think I'm going to go down for this?"

"Pay attention to me, Jacob," I whispered. "He's done. It's over." I focused my eyes on his, forcing him to look at me, to push the DA's words out of his mind.

"Who's the real victim here?" I heard Wickam say. "I'm the district attorney, for goodness' sake. This man came in here and threatened my life. It was self-defense."

"We'll sort it out later," Snow's voice came into the room. "For the time being, we've got a place for you down at the station."

Hearing the shuffle behind me and, most importantly, the click of the cuffs, I finally eased up on Jacob, getting to my feet and, after a second or two, I reached down and helped him to his feet.

"Look at me, Jacob," I said, looking him in the eyes, one hand on his shoulder. "It's over. Mission accomplished."

And it was.

34

One week later

A WEEK LATER, WICKAM WAS INDICTED, ALONG WITH Frank Hernandez, for conspiracy to murder, along with a whole list of other charges, including the murders of Dillon Harper, Brian McDaniel, David Young, Greg Sneed, Rachel Waldon, and Brenda Polaski. The evidence against them, culminating with the footage of Wickam delivering the donuts, was overwhelming. Detective Baker was extradited from Alaska and was given immunity and a place in the Witness Protection Program in return for her testimony, which, in itself, was damning. A trial date was set for September, but it was to be a formality as both men agreed to plead guilty in return for a sentence of twenty-five to life, which, for them, was better than a death sentence. It was about as good as it gets.

Jacob Harper re-upped, became a marine again, and last I heard was on a ship somewhere in the South China Sea.

Eddy McDaniel, relieved to know his son hadn't committed suicide, checked into a rehab program with Blake's help.

It was about a week later, and I was sitting in my usual spot on the couch in the living room when Amanda crept down the stairs after putting Jade to bed and slipped under my arm into her usual spot.

"You're quiet tonight," she said. "Is it another case already?"

"No, not at all," I said and reached up to stroke her hair. "I was just thinking about the last one."

"Surely you don't think you missed something."

I laughed. "That's why I've got you here, to make sure I don't."

"I think you're going to have to put me on the payroll."

"No chance," I said. "I couldn't afford you... No. It was just something about this case. Standing there in the room, Wickam was so certain he was going to get away with it. I don't know. Maybe he had more faith in Hernandez than he should've, or maybe Frank just saw the light. But once Hernandez turned on him, there wasn't a prayer left for that man. I mean, even without Hernandez's confession, there wouldn't have been much hope." I shook my head. "What I don't understand is how everything he did could have gone unnoticed for so long."

"Maybe that's because he didn't necessarily want it to go unnoticed," she said. "Just unpunished. Arrogance is a funny thing; it does funny things to people. Makes them feel... godlike?"

"Maybe," I said. "It's just... you know Jacob Harper's shotgun? Not the one he had with him in Wickam's office, but the one his brother borrowed to go hunting that night? That was the one thing that stuck in my craw. Where was it? They did find it, you know. Originally—so Detective Baker said—they found it behind the seat in Brian McDaniel's truck, but then it went missing. Guess where it turned up?"

"Only one place I can think of, but it sounds incredibly stupid."

"Or arrogant," I said. "See, that's what I mean. Wickam kept it. Why would he do that? He tried to feed Snow some line about it being an antique, and as far as that goes, he's right, but the provenance on that piece has more than a few holes in it for Wickam to claim rightful ownership. What kind of a person does that? If he wanted an antique shotgun, he more than had the means for it. It was just another nail in his proverbial coffin."

I felt her shrug against me. "As you said, arrogance, or maybe it was a trophy, something to remind him of how great he was, how smart, how much power he wielded."

I shook my head. "Keeping something like that is a whole different level of crazy."

"But not crazy enough, right?" she said, then added, "What exactly *was* he into, Harry?"

I laughed. "Hah, who knows? The TBI is still digging through it all... Drugs and guns, for sure." I shook my head. "He has money stashed away all over the Caribbean... Well, no matter what, he's done. He's going down for a long time."

"Good," she said. "I was just about getting to the end of my tether with this one."

I looked down at her. "Really, that's not like you, my love. Too much time on the road? Cleveland's only half an hour or so away."

"Each way," she corrected. "Don't think I haven't been keeping track. In fact." She sat up and turned around on the couch to face me. "I've got quite the log of extra hours you owe us, Harry Starke, and I think this seems like the perfect time for me to cash in."

"Oh, you're an accountant now, are you?"

She laughed. "If the shoe fits, I guess. But here's the deal, by my numbers, you owe me and our daughter at least one entire week, no cases, no work, no nothing."

"This sounds suspiciously like a vacation," I replied.

"Ah! See what a great detective you are? So..." She slipped back under my arm. "Where are you going to take us?"

I laughed. "As long as you two are there, anywhere sounds great to me."

"Just not Cleveland," she said.

"Hey." I laughed. "I just found all the best diners up there."

"Beach front," she said. "No. Mountains. Oh wait, what about an island?"

I listened to her rattle off her ideas, each one sounding better than the last, and settled back into the couch. She was right; it was time to get out of town for a while. The agency could survive seven days without me. Then again, I thought, it could probably even make it fourteen... or more.

"How about Mayaguana?" I asked. "It's... unique. It's unspoiled. The population is only two-hundred forty, last time I looked, and a third of those are school children."

"The Bahamas?" she replied. "Perfect! Wait, you looked?"

I smiled down at her and said, "I did."

Thank you for reading *Train Wreck* the twentieth book in the Harry Starke Novels. I hope you enjoyed it, if you did please help others find Blair Howards Books by leaving a few words about it in the form of a review.

Harry Starke Is here with his next case!
Order your copy of Dead Pool Book 21 today!

Enjoy Chapter One below . . .

May 9, 2022

Monday Morning

Victoria Blue wasn't exactly anti-social. Not in the sense that she stayed inside with the curtains drawn and the phones unplugged. But if she was pressed, she'd have to admit she was at least uninterested in being social. Kind of a funny change, really. As a girl she'd been the typical, almost stereotypical chatty, pigtailed, rope-skipping kid who didn't stop talking until she fell asleep. And even then, if the stories were true, she kept up the grinning and muttering during happy dreams.

It wasn't that anything particularly bad had happened to her either, driving her into her shell and making her keep the rest of the world at arm's length. No, it was more of a steady, consistent, only mildly irritating experience with people that had led her to slowly keeping her guard up.

She hit the button on the one-cup coffee machine in her kitchen, thinking, hardly for the first time, that Hilden Heights was not quite what she'd been led to believe. Sure, it was wealthy. One of the wealthiest neighborhoods in the area. But as the saying goes, money can't buy class.

Maybe that was too harsh. But as much as she hated to admit it, there was a glaring difference between old money and new money, and if anyone doubted that, all they had to do was drive around a few of the neighborhood streets and take a look at what new money could do. Pools, intricate landscaping, and too many cars to even fit in the multicar garages. Boats left out in driveways. It was funny; in a lot of ways, the new money wasn't entirely unlike neighborhoods with no money at all. The only difference was the cost of the items left out in the elements.

But that wasn't her concern. She knew very well that she was extremely fortunate to be born into the family she was and that it was through no effort of her own that she ended up in such a comfortable position. Even with her work, which she was proud to say supported her lifestyle without any of dad's, or grandma's, or great-grandpa's money, she would be doing just fine. Maybe that was just another blessing of wealth, though. Not every kid grew up with a computer, let alone multiple ones, and it had surely given her a jumpstart when she'd taken an interest in software engineering.

She was a quick study and had put the hours in, so sure, maybe she'd picked the Heights to be in what seemed like a familiar position, socio-economically speaking, but she also liked being able to just hunker down at home, do her work, create her programs, and be left alone for the most part. No harm, no foul, as her dad would've said.

You'll never get a man like that, her mom would've muttered.

But who needed a man when you could take care of yourself? And besides, she had Dipper.

She patted her thigh softly and the little black and brown Yorkshire Terrier stood up in his dog bed, stretching his front legs before trotting over to where she stood at the kitchen island.

Victoria pulled a thin rawhide chew from a bag in one of the cupboards and tucked it in her back pocket. Dipper immediately sat, attentive but not overly rambunctious, another thing she knew she had to be thankful for. Yorkies weren't known for their calm demeanor, but she'd hit the lottery with Dip.

The coffee maker let out its final gurgle and whoosh, and grabbing her laptop from the marble island, she took her work and her dog and stepped out through the sliding glass door into a screened-in porch, then onto a concrete patio. Off to her right, a small pool glittered in the morning light, the pool jets sending quiet arcs of water out to keep the salt and chlorine mixing. To her left was her workspace, at least on days like this. A solid roofed pergola, complete with an outdoor couch and round concrete table, awaited her.

Dipper skipped along at her side, eyeing the treat in her pocket as she walked over and set down her things. The sun was warm, though not hot enough to prevent her from getting a few hours of work done before she headed in for lunch. She handed the rawhide to Dip, who took it gingerly in his jaws and then circled the table a few times before finding what was apparently the perfect spot for snacking.

Maybe a ranch would've been wiser, she thought, glancing at the fence around her backyard. A lot more work, and Dip wouldn't be able to run quite so free—she'd heard more than one story about owls and hawks making a meal of small breeds like this—but it would at least give her a place she felt like she could relax. Here, the neighbors' roofs and windows were visible, despite the required extravagant space between homes, and even with her thick curtains, she always felt like she was just too exposed.

The feeling was only confirmed when she realized the bubbling of the deck jets wasn't the only water she could hear. A shape moved on the other side of the fence, casting a shadow through the slats and sending misty sprays of water into the air.

"Gotta get those flowers, don'tcha, Nel?" Victoria said under her breath just as a head poked up over the fence between her and her nearest neighbor's yard.

"Good morning, Vickie!" Nel Modesto called. "I thought I heard you out here."

Heard, or saw? Victoria thought. The situation was only made worse by the fact that she could see the woman, which only meant one thing. Nel Modesto was standing on one of the landscaping structures. Most of the homes, Victoria had noticed when house-shopping, had backyards that were more concrete than grass. Not that she had any right to complain, she supposed. But the Modestos had built themselves a kind of brick and concrete bench all around the perimeter of their backyard, then packed in enough potting soil and flowers to make God rethink the Garden of Eden. The fact it also allowed Nel to "unobtrusively" glance over her fence whenever she felt like it was certainly just a coincidence. Heavens no, folks in the Heights would never be that snoopy. Lordamercy.

"Morning, Nel," Victoria called, deciding it was pointless to request that Nel stop using the diminutive. "Vickie" made it sound like they were friends, good neighbors, confidants. If that's how Nel wanted folks to view them, well, it wasn't exactly Victoria's problem. "Thirsty flowers today?"

"Oh, these passion flowers," the woman said, stepping back down and out of sight, though her voice carried just fine, even with all the running water. "You'd never guess they were wildflowers with all the attention they demand. You know—"

Victoria groaned inwardly.

"This is actually one of two state flowers. Quite the fuss over it a while back. Most folks wanted the lily, but here we are."

Victoria mouthed the last four words along with Nel. She'd heard the story at least half a dozen times, and all she really wanted to do was get down to work. But, she supposed she couldn't fault the woman for trying to be friendly. It wasn't Nel's fault Victoria preferred Dipper to any human companion she'd ever had.

"The weather's been cool in the evenings yet," Victoria said, hoping to wind things up. "I'm sure you'll get it figured out. You've always got the perfect concoction to make them grow."

"Oh," Victoria heard Nel say. "You're flattering me. Mostly it's just water and sun, but now that you mention it, I do have a new plant food I've been wanting to tell you about. Let me see if I can find it in the garage."

Victoria watched the shadow move through the fence slats back toward the house. It was a childish move, but she also knew this was her chance to get back inside and avoid wasting a good forty-five minutes talking about soil nutrients with a woman she was only truly slightly acquainted with. Victoria closed her laptop and picked up her coffee, looking around for the dog.

At some point, he'd apparently given up the rawhide, an unusual choice for her little guy. Instead, he was standing over at the corner of the fence, stock-still, his attention rapt on something.

"Dip," she said, her voice barely above a whisper. She supposed she could leave him out, but Nel would be just as likely to come grab the dog and bring him to Victoria's door as anything. Just being a good neighbor and all, of course.

When the dog ignored her completely, Victoria put down her things and walked over to the fence. The lots on this side of the Heights were offset, meaning that while she and Nel shared a fence line, the home behind them actually was split down the middle, half butting up on Victoria's side and the other half on Nel's. Dipper, for his part, was staring right through the corner of the fence, meaning whatever had his attention was happening in Hattie Baker's backyard.

What that could be, however, was beyond Victoria. Hattie hadn't even reached thirty yet, and she was enjoying all the things that youth and new money could bring. Her favorite of which seemed to be sleeping until at least noon every day. But that didn't mean a partygoer hadn't decided to sleep in a lounger by the pool, or more likely, food had been left out on one of Hattie's garishly expensive platters.

Silver platters but not land, or stocks, or literally anything else, Victoria thought. Grandma would roll over in her grave.

She walked over to the dog and, fully aware that she was doing exactly what she'd just been irked by Nel for, Victoria tried to peek through the wooden slats and see what had Dipper so attentive.

At first it looked like nothing. Hattie's backyard was empty besides the overflow of pool furniture. The house looked dark; its curtains drawn. Then, just beyond the edge of her little slit of vision, she thought she saw it. Someone was in the pool. Early morning floats weren't exactly Hattie's style, but as she'd been keen to let everyone know, despite the ridiculous size of the pool, it was heated and could be used "even on the most frigid Tennessee evening; it's practically a giant hot tub!"

Victoria almost dismissed it and turned back inside, but something in her brain registered the scene as being off, just a little wonky, as her dad would've said. Like a state having two state flowers, as Nel would be saying shortly if Victoria didn't get back inside.

But still, she couldn't help but be curious, and before she realized she was doing it, she'd pulled a chair over and stepped up on it, trying to keep her head low while at least figuring out what exactly was going on in Hattie's yard. The woman always played music when she was out, and she was rarely out alone. And again, it was barely the crack of ten AM.

Victoria's eyes widened as she took in the pool, and then she quietly, albeit shakily, stepped down from the chair and scooped up her dog. The work could wait. Nel could wait indefinitely. Victoria needed to make a phone call. This was entirely not the thing she was anxious about getting involved in when she'd first moved to the Heights, but it certainly did nothing to cancel out her concerns about being too close to people. Now she'd be involved. There'd be more questions. Interviews. Gossip. More than anything, gossip.

But, she thought, an anonymous call might at least buy her some time. If nothing else, it would keep the cops from showing up at her door at the same time they did Hattie's. At least, she hoped so.

Whatever her own concerns were, she couldn't in good conscience just go back inside and wait. Hattie Baker, even if she did sleep in and did listen to music too loud and did buy platters instead of real estate, didn't deserve to have her dead body floating in the pool until someone happened by in the next who knew how many hours.

Victoria slipped back through the porch and pulled the sliding door closed behind her, Dipper in the crook of her arm and her coffee and laptop still out on the table. She took a deep breath. How to even begin? "I'd like to report a death"?

READY TO READ THE REST?

GET THE FULL VERSION OF DEAD POOL BOOK 21 TODAY!

Short Stories and Novellas

Buried Secrets(Harry Starke)

The Painted Lady(Kate Gazzara)

Stand Alone

Hunter's Moon(Kate & Harry)

Series

The Harry Starke Genesis Series

9 Books in Series as of 2025

The Harry Starke Series

26 Books in Series as of October 2025

The Lt. Kate Gazzara Murder Files

22 Books in Series as of October 2025

Randall And Carver Mysteries

4 Books in Series as of October 2025

The Peacemaker Series

3 Books in Series as of October 2025

The O'Sullivan Chronicles: Civil War Series

5 Books in Series as of October 2025

Science Fiction From Blair C. Howard

The Sovereign Star Series

7 Books in Series as of October 2025

also available in German

The Predecessors Series

ABOUT THE AUTHOR

Blair Howard is the international best-selling author of more than seventy novels that span the worlds of gritty detective fiction, espionage thrillers, sweeping historicals, and hard-science military space opera. A Royal Air Force veteran and former journalist, he draws upon a rich background of service and storytelling to breathe life into unforgettable characters such as ex-cop turned private eye Harry Starke, and the fiercely determined homicide detective Lt. Kate Gazzara, who breaks her own trail as the head of a serious-crimes unit.

Under his sci-fi pen name Blair C. Howard, he expands his reach into the cosmos with the Sovereign Stars saga—an epic journey born from his lifelong love of the heavens, and the Predecessors hard science fiction trilogy. Whether unraveling a brutal crime scene or commanding starships in interstellar conflict, his stories are propelled by relentless pacing, vivid realism, and a watchful eye for justice.

Visit www.blairhowardbooks.com.
Email: BlairHoward@BlairHowardBooks.com

You can also find Blair Howard on Social Media